D1266939

# *The*
# SECRET
# WITHIN

Also by
Theresa Martin Golding

*Kat's Surrender*

# The
# SECRET
# WITHIN

### Theresa Martin Golding

## BOYDS MILLS PRESS

Text copyright © 2002 by Theresa Martin Golding

Published by Boyds Mills Press, Inc.
A Highlights Company
815 Church Street
Honesdale, Pennsylvania   18431
Printed in China
Visit our Web site at www.boydsmillspress.com

Publisher Cataloging-in-Publication Data

Golding, Theresa Martin
    The secret within / by Theresa Martin Golding.—1st ed.
[240]p.  :  cm.
Summary: A teenage girl, whose father is involved in criminal activity, fights to
survive an abusive homelife and the loneliness that seems to have no end.
ISBN 1-56397-995-0
1. Abused teenagers — Fiction — Juvenile literature. 2. Loneliness in adoles-
cence — Fiction — Juvenile literature. 3. Fathers and daughters — Fiction —
Juvenile literature. I. Title.

[F]   21   2002   CIP
2001093641


First edition, 2002
The text of this book is set in 13-point Berkeley Book.

10 9 8 7 6 5 4 3

To my siblings, Kathie, Jim, Paul, Greg, and
Eileen. And to their spouses, Bruce, Sheila,
Peggy, Betty, and Dave, who are more than just
family, but my best friends as well.
And as promised, to my mother and
father, great parents in every way, who bear
absolutely no resemblance to Vinnie and
Leila Chambers in this book.
Finally, to Gil, Jennifer, Michael,
and Mary Kathryn, because you are
a part of everything I do.

# CHAPTER 1

Carly raced down the cement sidewalk, her feet bare and her hair tangled and filled with sand. The sun had been up only a few hours, but the pavement was already turning hot as a griddle. Here and there a small oasis of cool grass sprouted before a house's front stoop, but Carly dared not stop. Broken flip-flops in her hand, she concentrated on the sidewalk, running hard, but carefully, picking her way around cracks, crumbling squares, and the ubiquitous white pebbles that spilled from the yards of the beach houses that lined the street.

Halfway up 33rd Avenue, she saw Frankie Marzano. She slowed her pace, but it was too late to take a detour. He was standing in the middle of the sidewalk waiting for her to approach.

Carly's heart was pounding. She could feel the sweat trickling down the back of her neck. Get out of the way, Frankie, please get out of the way, she thought. Carly crossed to the other side of the street, the blacktop even hotter than the cement, the soles of her feet cooking with each step.

Frankie was wearing a new pair of Nikes, laced tight, and a faded pair of baggy shorts that seemed danger- ously close to slipping off his skinny hips and falling below his knees. It was early August, and his bare chest was tanned a deep brown. He sprinted across the street to stand in Carly's way.

"Cool threads," Frankie sneered, tugging at Carly's worn T-shirt and eyeing her up and down. "And what's that perfume you're wearing? Eau de wet sand?"

Carly tried to pass him on the right and then on the left. Each time she moved, he jumped in front of her to block her path.

Normally, Carly just stood quietly until he got bored with making fun of her. That's what she did at school, through all of eighth grade, in the cafeteria, in the audi- torium, in study hall. But today, Frankie seemed revved up and she couldn't wait it out. She was way late, dan- gerously late even, and she was beginning to panic.

Carly felt the fire in her feet traveling up through her body and she exploded. She bolted past Frankie, knock- ing him sideways, and took off up 33rd Avenue. She heard him cursing her as she ran, but that was nothing compared to what she would face when she got home.

At the corner of 33rd and Atlantic Avenues, just across the street from her house, Carly paused beneath a tree to catch her breath. She didn't want to go in panting, and she needed to think of some kind of decent excuse. The house looked quiet. At least he wasn't peering out the window or pacing the sidewalk in front of the candy store.

Carly yanked at a length of her long, brown hair and twirled it around her fingers. She stared at the drab, quiet candy shop. She had been in such a rush to get here and now she couldn't bring herself to go in. She hugged her arms to her chest and took a deep breath. It felt like a dozen crabs were crawling around inside her, pinching their way up the sides of her stomach and then back down again.

A pair of cool hands slipped over Carly's eyes. "Guess who?"

"Get off!" Carly twisted away, arms raised in front of her face. She stumbled backward over the curb and fell into the street. She unclenched her jaw when she saw that it was only Aileen, her next-door neighbor.

"Whoa. You're a bit jumpy." Aileen reached a hand down and pulled Carly to her feet. "You okay?"

"Fine. I can't really talk now, Aileen." Carly quickly scanned the windows of her house, then ducked behind the tree. "I gotta go."

"In trouble again?" Aileen played with a big wad of chewing gum in her mouth, pulling a long, droopy string through her teeth and wrapping it around her finger.

"I don't know what you're talking about." Carly felt the sweat beading on her upper lip and quickly wiped it away, the salty taste seeping into her mouth and drying out her throat.

"Yeah, right." Aileen popped the bubble-gum ring from her finger back into her mouth.

Carly narrowed her eyes and bit on her thumbnail.

"So what kind of trouble is it?" Aileen chewed like a cow, opening and closing her big mouth with a loud *glop, glop*.

"There's *no* trouble," Carly insisted, pressing herself flat against the trunk of the tree. But there was going to be. Her father had sent her out this morning in search of *The Trenton Times*, not a hard paper to find in this South Jersey resort town. He rarely let her out alone, and he timed all her errands. She had raced to the beach, hoping to steal just a few minutes there before swinging by the local newsstand and racing home again. But the ocean was so beautiful, draped with a soft morning mist, that she not only forgot the time but lost the coins for the paper in the sand as well.

"I'm not stupid, you know. You don't have to pretend with me."

"I'm not pretending anything!" Carly turned to leave, but Aileen grabbed her arm.

She blew a large pink bubble that popped inches from Carly's face. "Then what's the rush? Why don't you come and hang out at my house for a while? I got a new CD we could listen to."

Carly knew she'd need an invisibility cloak to walk past her house in the company of Aileen. Her father disapproved of most teenagers, and Aileen was at the top of his list. She had a small, silver ball earring in her right nostril that sparkled in the summer sun and both ears were pierced in numerous places. Her kinky red hair flew out wildly from her head and bounced on her shoulders like coiled ribbons whenever she moved.

All her clothes were either too large or too small, and it wasn't uncommon to see her strutting up the street, singing aloud or angrily talking to herself, complaining about some injustice or another.

Though she was three years older than Carly, they rode the same bus to school, and Aileen frequently pushed into the seat with Carly, chatting away about her nails, her mousy math teacher, or whatever else popped into her head. Carly wasn't ever sure if Aileen was talking to her or just thinking aloud. She couldn't always follow the conversation. It was like trying to watch television when somebody else had the remote, changing the channel every few minutes. Just when Carly would start to become interested in what she was saying, Aileen would change the subject and lose her. And she was nosy too, asking personal questions that made Carly's throat close up and her hands clench tightly against her backpack. Mostly, Carly only listened with one ear and gazed out the bus window, staring at all the lucky people free from the confines of school and home.

"So what do you think, you wanna come over?" Today Aileen was wearing a tie-dyed tank top that was stretched to the limit, barely covering half her stomach, and a faded pair of jeans that were several inches too long for her legs. She leaned into the tree and set to work on her gum again, expertly looping it on her index finger, the color all the more pink against the black of her fingernails.

"I can't, okay? I have to work the register today."

Aileen swung her head toward the store. One of her red curls got stuck in the gum in the corner of her mouth and she worked at getting it free. "Yeah. Looks reeeeal busy over there. The line's just bustin' out the door. You better rush on over."

Carly looked across the street at the empty sidewalk. Her parents ran a candy-and-gift shop out of the first floor of their home, an old weather-beaten Victorian, three stories high. They had a great location for the shop, right on a busy corner, only two blocks from the beach and the boardwalk. But after two years, they still didn't seem to have many customers. It was the longest they had ever lived in any one place. Carly would tap dance on the street corner dressed as a peppermint saltwater taffy if it would help business, but she doubted it would.

The candy shop was turning out to be a failure like all her father's other ventures. And after they failed, the family would pack up and move. It didn't matter to Carly where they went, because it was always the same—old house, old chores, tired street, brown brick school, a few strip malls and fast food restaurants down the road.

Oceanside was different. She knew it from that first moment when she and her parents had driven their packed car into town and parked on the sandy street. Her father had been in a good mood and held her hand as they walked toward the beach, excited to show her the ocean.

Carly had been speechless when she climbed over the dune and saw the huge expanse of sparkling ocean in front of her. When she first inhaled the salt spray, it drifted down through her chest and settled over her heart. She had been caught, and she happily became entangled in the rhythms of the place. There was high season and low, calm waters and nor'easters. Ocean temperatures and tides rose and fell with soothing regularity.

Carly peeked out from behind the tree and scanned the windows of her house again. "I just got stuff to do, Aileen, okay? I gotta go home." She darted from behind the tree and into the street.

"I'll stop by your house later, then," Aileen called.

"No!" Carly whirled around and stopped in the middle of the street, but Aileen was already walking away, hoisting up her oversized pants and singing in her self-absorbed way.

Carly took a deep breath and headed for her house.

# Chapter 2

Carly peered in the window of the candy shop and, seeing no one, eased the door open. There was a little bell inside about three-quarters of the way up the frame and she stuck her hand in first to grab it and then slid her body in after. The ice-cold air shocked her sweaty skin and she felt the goose bumps rising on her back. She was inching the door closed, the little bell cupped in her hand, when the door to the back room flew open. Carly jumped, knocking the door shut, and that annoying little tinkle filled the shop.

Her father walked slowly toward her. "Do you know what time it is, Carly?" He spoke calmly, but she could see the color rising in dark, mottled splotches on his face.

He was a large man, over six feet tall, with a build that had probably once been athletic but was now turning soft and stocky. His jet-black hair was wild and kinky. It curled up not only around his head but all over his body, like a troublesome weed that had escaped and taken root.

"Carly? I asked you a question, dear." There was a fake sweetness in his voice, like maple syrup on plastic pancakes. It all ran off when you tried to take your first bite.

She tried to gauge his anger, but it was difficult. Sometimes it exploded violently, and other times fizzled away to a silent brooding. There was no telling which way this one would go.

Mr. Chambers slammed his hand down on the counter. "Did you hear me?" he shouted, dropping all pretense of sweetness. "When I ask you a question, I want an answer!"

Carly moved away from the glass door and back behind the counter. If he was going to blow, he would have to do it without her help. All her answers were wrong, and it seemed sometimes that her very voice was the thing that set him off. She had long ago taken silence as her ally. It was always there when she needed it. She drew it now, like a shade between them.

Her father rounded the corner of the counter. "Where's the paper, Carly? Where's the paper? I need that paper. Where is it?" His voice rose and fell, half pleading, half threatening. She couldn't tell if he was going to cry or smack her. She backed up against the wall and grabbed the broom from beside the cash register. It always made her feel better to be holding something, anything. Her body tensed and she felt the throb of old wounds.

"Look at me, Carly," he commanded, so close she could feel his breath on her face.

Carly looked up but refused to meet his eyes.

15

She stared at his green shirt, counted the buttons.

"I'm only going to ask you nicely one more time." He clenched his right hand into a fist, four white-knuckle peaks above the forest of black hair. Carly focused on the edge of his collar where it was unraveling, green thread hanging down, a creeping vine.

"Did you get the newspaper or not?"

She shook her head ever so slightly. He slammed his fist on the counter again and cursed her. "I can't believe it! One lousy newspaper. That's all I asked you to get. Where were you?"

The phone in the back room rang. Carly heard her mother answer it in her quick, whispering voice. She appeared in the office doorway, her small dark eyes darting to Carly. "Vinnie. Vinnie, the phone's for you."

He stood staring at Carly, jaws clenched, left hand gripping his forehead. His chest was heaving up and down, a rumbling volcano beneath the carpet of green shirt. Carly twisted her hands back and forth on the worn broom handle.

Mrs. Chambers stood rigidly by the office, her right hand curled around the door frame. "Vinnie, come get the phone," she said pleadingly.

He glared at Carly, unmoving. Carly stood perfectly still, holding her breath.

"Please, Vinnie," Mrs. Chambers begged. "Take the call. I think it's important. I'll take care of everything out here."

He finally turned away, but as he reached the end of the counter, he grabbed a display bowl of mints and flung it across the room. It crashed against the wall and shattered, mints and glass raining to the floor.

"She's worthless," he said and pushed past his wife into the back room.

Carly dropped the broom beside the register and leaned against the glass counter. She stared down at the rows of chocolates, her head in her hands. The worst thing of all was, he was right. She was worthless. She should have gotten the stupid newspaper first and then gone for a visit to the beach. Newspapers don't get lost in the sand. She never thought of these things until after she messed up, until after she ruined everything. Carly slid the case door open and let out a fly that was flinging itself in a frenzy against the glass.

Her mother came toward her, a stack of empty one pound boxes in her hand. "You didn't get the paper?" she asked.

"No," Carly answered, sliding the case door shut with a bang. "I didn't."

"You were gone so long," her mother said softly. "Where were you? You can tell me the truth."

She would have loved to tell her mother the truth. To sit curled in her lap like she did when she was younger and whisper secrets while her mother stroked her hair. They were only little girl secrets, but somehow her father always managed to find out. He knew about the smooth little black rock she had found in the garden and carried in her pocket for good luck. He knew how afraid she was of the wolf in her Little Red Riding Hood storybook. He discovered the hiding place of her treasure box filled with rings from the bubble-gum machine and small toys found inside cereal boxes. He knew about every one and used them against her when he wanted something. So she learned to keep all her secrets locked away inside. He couldn't find them. He couldn't touch them.

"You can tell me, Carly," her mother pressed.

"I tried to find the paper. I really tried," Carly lied. "I went to a whole bunch of stores, but none of them had *The Trenton Times*. That happens sometimes, you know. Maybe the truck broke down."

"How did you get that sand all over you?"

Carly rubbed the back of her thigh and felt the grains tumble down her leg to the floor.

"Those kids got me with their sand balls again," Carly began. Frankie and his friends had once pelted her with hard balls of sand that stung like exploding slaps and left her gritty and sore. "It was right after I came out of the Wawa. They were on the corner and they had all this sand in a wagon. I tried to run, but I was only wearing my flip-flops and they broke." It scared her sometimes, how easily the lies came now, how real they seemed once she told them.

Carly's mother set the boxes on the counter and gave Carly's shoulder a small pat. "All right. Don't worry about it. But when he comes out, stay out of his way, okay? I'll tell him what happened. How about you help me get this mess cleaned up. We'll be opening up soon."

Carly sighed and looked around the small shop. They had only one glass display counter that ran the length of the room. Opposite it was a wall lined with shelves where customers could pick their own prepackaged candies—saltwater taffy, fudge, and colorful tins of gumdrops. There were little trinkets too, souvenirs for people with money to waste, plastic starfish and necklaces made of seashells.

Her mother grabbed the broom and began to sweep the glass and mints from the gray tile floor. She was never still, always wiping or cleaning something. She was never more than three feet from a squirt bottle and rag. She wiped down the cash register and door handles after every customer and kept a supply of toothbrushes under the counter for getting the dirt out of the cracks in the floor. On those few occasions when she was sitting, her hands moved continuously with knitting or mending and her leg shook with a nervous energy that, if it could be harnessed, would easily power all the electrical appliances in the house. She was not much taller than five feet and so skinny that she could stand behind a telephone pole and not be seen. At thirteen, Carly probably had four inches and fifteen pounds on her already.

"Maybe we'll get a chance to make some iced tea today, you and me, and sit out in the yard for a bit." Her mother spoke quietly with a sidelong glance at the office door. Her dark tangled hair hung halfway down her back and the bangs she wore in front were always in her eyes. She was constantly flipping them back with her right hand or throwing her head back in a quick, jerking motion, but the hair always crept down to obstruct her line of vision. She was peering at Carly through the tangled strands as she swept. "What do you think?"

"Yeah. Maybe," Carly answered, but she knew it wouldn't happen. Her mother was full of plans that were always hours or days out of reach. Maybe tonight we'll go out for ice cream. Maybe tomorrow we'll go see that movie. But he always needed her for something. The books had to be balanced, the boxes made up, the cellar work, whatever that was, had to get done. Carly knew that her mother needed to dream, just as she did, so she willingly played the "maybe" game and never complained that their plans, all neglected, always died.

Carly began to pick up the scattered mints from the floor. She lingered over those by the door, gazing long- ingly out into the sun-drenched street. Families were on their way to the ocean, parents dragging beach chairs and sunburned toddlers, children grasping their buckets and sailboats. All of them gliding lazily to the shore, warm and smiling, fit and relaxed. With the air conditioner in the shop constantly droning, it was like watching a big screen TV with the volume on mute. Children cried and laughed in silence and cars motored up to the traffic light without a rumble. Day after day, confined to the shop, she made up the words that came out of their mouths and created their days and dreamed of their lives long after they had passed the window by.

"Carly?" Her mother was standing over her. "Are you taking a nap down there or what?"

"Just a minute." Carly caught sight of the fly crawling up and down the glass door. She opened the door to shoo it out, but it flew the wrong way and buzzed back into the store. She got the dustpan and brush and began to sweep up the small pile her mother had made.

They heard the phone in the back room slam down.

"Quick," her mother whispered, "run up to your room for a bit. I'll finish up."

They heard his chair scrape back from the desk. Carly sprinted through the small shop and up two flights of stairs to her room.

# CHAPTER 3

Carly paced the floor of her small attic bedroom. It was eight o'clock in the evening and the sky over the bay would soon be turning brilliant shades of orange, purple, and blue. She turned off the small fan that droned in the corner by her bed, silently cracked opened her door and stood motionless for several minutes, listening. The air in the room was as thick as warm Jell-O and her clothes clung damply to her body. The staircase to the living area below was dark. All was silent. After their ritual evening coffee, her parents always retreated to the cellar or the office or to the living room for one of their favorite television shows. It was the moment Carly looked forward to every night. She locked her door, and carefully removed the screen from the window.

She climbed out and sat on the sloping roof. The first night she had done this, it was only to escape the stifling heat of her room. She had lain there on her back, admiring the night sky, listening to the sounds that floated up to her: a car door slamming, a couple laughing, the faint buzz of a Phillies game on the radio from someone's open window. Then a bird in the backyard tree, somehow disturbed from its evening rest, began noisily complaining and fluttering about. Staring at the tree, she had gotten an idea. She began to crawl along the roofline. Halfway across, a patch of loose tiles moved under her weight, and she swallowed a scream as she almost tumbled from the roof. She caught her breath and moved more carefully, checking for other dangerous spots. She soon reached the corner of the roof, where the branches of the tree rested against the house. It looked so easy. She hesitated, but not more than five minutes. She would only go for a little while and they would never notice she was gone. And they didn't.

She had felt so light and free, like a helium balloon carried by the wind. She wasn't on an errand and she wasn't being timed. She glided slowly down the streets, taking in all the houses, savoring the sounds and smells that drifted out of each one. She went up on the board-walk and mingled with the crowds. She crossed the sand and stood in the darkness at the ocean's edge, feeling within her chest the boom of each wave as it crashed against the beach and rushed, foaming, around her ankles. She went home finally, her heart thumping wildly as she approached the house. She climbed the tree and crept like a cat across the roof and into her room. It was as quiet and empty as she had left it. The excitement that pounded through her veins was almost painful, like an electric current coursing her body. Now, she went out almost every night and stayed as

23

long as she dared. Her parents, busy with their own affairs, never knew that she was gone.

Carly sat for a moment on the edge of the roof, watching the deepening color of the sky and savoring the feel of the evening breeze. Even though she had been sneaking out for weeks now, the excitement was still there, and she felt it tickle its way up through her stomach and into her chest. She had a friend on the boardwalk now, and even a small job, sort of. She didn't want to be late. Carly crawled across the roof, shimmied her way into the tree, then dropped noiselessly into the backyard. She ran the two blocks to the boardwalk.

The boardwalk was a raised platform of wooden planks, nailed end to end, which stretched for several miles over the sand along the edge of the beach. Ramps descended from it every street or two and on warm summer nights the people flowed up them, scrubbed clean of sand, their skin taut and red from a day on the beach. Gone were the smells of sunblock lotion, turkey sandwiches, and wet sand and the sounds of lifeguard whistles and squawking gulls. The aroma of the night boardwalk was of tar and wood, salt spray and popcorn, funnel cake and pizza and fries. Shops of every kind lined its western side: gift shops, bookstores, ice-cream stands, T-shirt shops. There was an old movie theater with a brightly lit marquee and a black-lettered sign in the ticket booth window that promised "We Are Air Conditioned."

Several amusement piers jutted out from the main boardwalk and were crammed with rides. Roller coasters rumbled, the scrambler hummed, bumper cars crashed, and pre-recorded screams drifted from the haunted house. Small children squealed as they went round and round beeping the horns of fire engines or stroking the plastic manes of the horses on the merry-go-round. The lights of the giant Ferris wheel loomed above them all, swaying and sparkling against the dark and distant sky.

There were also games of chance, skee-ball and balloon darts, water guns and bingo. Long lines snaked around the compact miniature golf courses and filled the arcades. And everywhere there were people, from newborns to teenagers to the elderly in wheelchairs.

Carly went straight to the old blue newsstand in the center of the boardwalk at 32nd Street and climbed up onto the round stool set just outside its open side door.

"Hey, Eddie," Carly said, as he made change for a customer.

"Carly! Man, am I glad to see you. We've been busy tonight. I need you already." Eddie reached down and pulled up a gray, plastic bucket half full of coins and handed it to Carly. "Can you do it?"

"Sure," Carly answered. Eddie's newsstand was her home base on the boardwalk. There was always a stool there for her and loose change for sodas and ice cream. She liked helping Eddie out, sorting the coins while they talked and played their people-watching games. They would guess at customers' occupations after they'd left the stand—lawyer, hairdresser, mob boss—and try to pinpoint hometowns by the accents—the nasal New Yorkers and the halting French Canadians were the easiest.

A tall, thin man glided up to the stand and bought *The Philadelphia Inquirer.*

"Basketball player," Carly said, as the man drifted back into the throng.

"Musician," Eddie countered. "Didn't you see those hands?"

Carly looked down at her own chapped hands, deftly sliding the quarters into the cylindrical paper counters from the bank. "But he was so tall. Anybody that tall must be a basketball player."

"Too old. He was in his forties, an old man like me." Eddie pulled a handkerchief from his front shirt pocket and wiped the beaded perspiration from his face.

"Okay, then," Carly said. "He was a professional basketball player who got too old, and when his contract expired, no teams wanted to pick him up. So he went back to his first love, music, and now he plays the violin with the Philadelphia Orchestra."

Eddie smiled. "Yeah, probably. You know, you could get a job in Hollywood writing movie scripts." He took a handful of change out of his apron and dumped it into the bucket. "Any air out there at all tonight?"

"A little bit," Carly said, working on the nickels. "It's pretty nice, actually."

"Could've fooled me," Eddie sighed, mopping his brow again.

There was a whole different weather system inside that tiny box of a newsstand, and mostly it was just hot.

Eddie, sitting on his cushioned stool and reclining against the back wall, filled up almost the entire space. He was quite fat, probably three hundred pounds or more, and his stomach, like an overfilled water balloon, covered the length of his lap. He had a window-like opening in the front of the newsstand where he could see his customers and a small wooden ledge where he kept his best selling papers. He wore a pocketed apron for collecting bills and change. When it got too full, he dumped the excess coins into the bucket. There were bundled stacks of the late editions of the papers piled to the left of his stool. All the magazines he carried were on racks just in front of the stand. Eddie could do a steady business the entire night without moving anything except his eyes and his hands.

A man in a trench coat with a cap pulled low over his eyes stopped at the stand. A well-dressed woman stood with him, her hand in his. They wanted *U. S. News and World Report*. Carly jumped off the stool and pulled it from the bottom of the rack. It wasn't one of Eddie's best sellers. They paid and wandered off.

"Spies," Carly whispered.

"Definitely spies," Eddie agreed. "Either that or he likes to be prepared for rain."

Carly hated the rain. There was no room for her inside the newsstand and she worried that, if they didn't dry by morning, her wet clothes and damp hair would get her caught.

Eddie smiled at her and tossed her a mint from the supply he kept in his apron pocket. As she sucked on

27

the candy and stacked the coins, she thought of the first time she had ever met Eddie. Surprisingly, she had Frankie Marzano to thank. She had been sitting on a bench on the ocean side of the boardwalk, watching the crowds, when she had spied Frankie and a couple of his friends strutting her way. Frankie didn't see her at first. He was too busy bothering other people. He and his friends would tap ladies on the shoulder, then look the other way. They pulled girls' ponytails and knocked popcorn boxes out of their hands. They stopped in front of Eddie's newsstand and pretended to be interested in the papers. They started flinging them, like paperboys serving a route. Eddie was too fat and slow to do anything but yell at them. When they started emptying the magazines off the racks, Carly couldn't stand it anymore. She had seen the same thing happen to the contents of her backpack too many times. She began to quietly retrieve the scattered papers and magazines and pile them behind the stand.

When Frankie finally saw her, the shock of her being up on the boardwalk momentarily froze him. Carly wasn't worried that she had been spotted. It was a big boardwalk and she knew she could outrun them all. It was her only talent, honed from years of sprinting home from errands to beat the clock and avoid the back of her father's hand. But she hadn't noticed that Mark Rossi and Justin Renfroe had circled around behind her. There was nowhere to run.

"Ladies and Gentlemen! May I have your attention please!" Frankie shouted. He began pretending that he was the announcer for the boardwalk freak show and Carly and the newspaperman were the stars. He made fun of her stringy hair and her worn clothes, her skinny legs and her freckles. People started looking at her. Carly couldn't stand that. She moved a few steps toward the newspaper stand and tried to squeeze in the door. Eddie shoved some papers out of the way, but it was useless. She just looked more ridiculous than ever, half in half out, *The New York Post* spilling around her feet. Eddie grabbed his cell phone then, and loudly pretended he was calling the police. Frankie and his friends yelled some final insults and ran away. Carly had picked up the rest of the papers and magazines, and Eddie gave her some money to go buy a couple of sodas. They had been friends ever since.

Carly crunched the sliver of mint left in her mouth. Her stomach growled.

"Wow!" Eddie exclaimed. "Was that you? It is getting kind of late. Are you hungry?"

Carly was running her fingers through the pennies in the bucket. She always saved the pennies for last. "Yeah, I am kind of hungry," she answered. Actually, she was starving. Her father remained so angry about the newspaper from this morning that she had been banned from the dinner table. She didn't tell Eddie that, or anything about her family. Her father had trained her early in family privacy. "What happens in this house, stays in this house. Don't be one of those fools who hangs out their dirty laundry for the whole world to see." Of all his rules, this one was the easiest to follow. She didn't want anyone to see what went on inside her house.

"What do you feel like eating?"

"Anything," Carly answered. She could've eaten a cow.

"How about pizza?" he asked, taking change from a customer and dropping it in his apron pocket.

"Pizza sounds good."

"Whew!" Eddie waved his hand in front of his face and stared at the disappearing figure of his last customer.

"I think she works in a perfume factory," Carly laughed.

"Yeah, and she fell into one of the vats." Eddie coughed. "That stench was enough to take my appetite away."

Carly raised her eyebrows and smiled at him.

"Hey, hey, no funny looks," Eddie complained. "I did lose my appetite once, you know. I think it was for an hour or so one afternoon back in 1974. Here." Eddie pulled some bills from his apron pocket. "Go to Margo's and get that pizza. Get me a large Diet Coke too and get yourself something to drink."

Carly slipped the money into the front pocket of her jeans and headed up the boardwalk toward Margo's Pizza. She chewed on her lower lip as she walked, wondering if Nick would be working tonight.

# CHAPTER 4

"Yo, Angela! Two Cokes, two Sprites for table four." Margo pointed at the waiting drinks then slid the big wooden paddle in the oven and turned the pizza. Her eyes took in every movement in the place, and her body did a kind of fast-food ballet all night, turning from oven to counter to register, dipping for dropped change, reaching for the top shelves.

Carly slid onto the corner stool at the end of the counter, her back to the ocean, and watched the show. Like most of the pizza places on the boardwalk, Margo's had no door, but was entirely open to the boardwalk on one side. The counter ran down the left side of the room, and all the cooking was done behind it. A row of simple booths was attached to the right wall. A few dusty posters were hung here and there depicting life in old Italy.

Margo rang up a customer, threw a pizza in the oven and, with half a turn, stood in front of Carly. "Carly! How are you, honey?"

"Good," Carly said, her hands holding the lip of the counter.

"Is that Eddie behaving himself?"

Carly nodded and smiled.

"Well, what's he hungry for tonight? The usual?" Margo's brown hair was drawn back in a ponytail, but several loose, damp strands hung down the sides of her face.

"Yes, please," Carly answered.

"Large pepperoni and a large Diet Coke. Coming right up." Margo filled a cup with soda and slid it in front of Carly. "Here you go, sweetheart. Have a drink while you're waiting."

Carly reached into her pocket for the folded up bills Eddie had given her.

"No, no," Margo said. "Put that back. That one's on the house."

"Thank you," Carly said, but Margo was already down the other end, checking the pizzas, spreading the sauce, taking the orders.

Margo was at the register with a customer when Nick came in, loose white T-shirt and baggy pants, his baseball cap turned backward on his head. Carly shrunk into the corner and lowered her head. Nick was one of the more decent guys in her class. He would actually say hello if he passed her in the hall or on the street and even though that wasn't exactly conversation, it was more talk than she had with most of the other kids. He was a super baseball player and the vice-president of their class. He could easily have been mean to her or ignored her. That would have been normal. That would have put him in the majority.

"Hey, Mom," Nick said, leaning across the counter and giving her a quick kiss on the cheek.

"Hey, Nicky. How'd it go tonight?"

"Great. Four to one. I almost had a shutout, but they scored one in the last inning."

"Way to go, Nicky." Margo gave him a congratulatory swat on the side of the head, leaving some floury fingerprints on his dark baseball cap.

"Need some help?" Nick asked, ducking under the counter.

"Yeah, sure could," Margo sighed, brushing the damp strands of hair back from her face. There were a few ceiling fans droning overhead, but they were as effective against the heat of the ovens as a bucket and shovel are against the rising tide. Margo drained half a cup of ice water and handed Nick a white apron.

"Nicky, why don't you take care of Carly down there. She's waiting on Eddie's pizza in number three. It should only be five more minutes or so."

Nick turned and saw Carly. "Hi," he said quickly and turned back toward his mom, whispering something.

"Go on, go on," Margo said. "See if she needs a refill on her drink."

Carly wanted to melt into the seat, to drip between the boards below, to drop unnoticed into the sand. When Margo and Nick turned their backs to the counter, filling drinks from the dispenser, Carly decided it was a good time to visit the restroom in the rear. She quickly closed the door, slipped the lock into place, and leaned back against the wall, sweating.

She pulled a length of toilet paper off the roll and held it in her hands, squeezing and rolling it into a damp wad.

There was a sudden bang and Carly jumped. But it was only the door to the closet that adjoined the restroom.

"Where are they?" She heard Nick's muffled voice through the wall. The walls were thin and his head was probably just a foot or two from hers. Carly held her breath.

"Top shelf, right," she heard Margo answer.

"I don't see them."

There were some shuffling noises. It sounded as though Margo was in the closet with Nick now, moving things around. Carly wondered if her pizza was done. She could just put the money on the counter, grab the pizza, and leave.

"Why don't you, Nick?" she heard Margo say. "Just walk her back to the newsstand or something."

"Mom, no way. Lay off," he answered.

Carly felt her stomach flip, and she crossed her arms over her chest.

"Why not?" Margo pressed. "It wouldn't kill you."

"Mom, you don't understand. She's a total dork. And even if I did, it would feel totally weird. She doesn't even talk, ever. What am I supposed to do, have a conversation with the pizza?"

"Ah, here they are," Margo said, banging something against the wall. "I just think it would be nice, that's all."

"Forget it," Nick said. "She's just one of those weird

people who. . ." The closet door banged shut and Carly could hear no more. Someone was jiggling the handle of the restroom door.

"Just a minute," Carly said weakly. She had taught herself not to cry several years ago, and she was sure that lack of use had dried up her reservoir of tears. But in their place was a dammed up river of lava, and she felt it now, searing her chest. She ran the water in the sink until it was ice cold, then splashed it on her face. She checked herself quickly in the small mirror; pasty white skin, a smattering of freckles, small green eyes— the face of a dork. Carly walked back to her stool at the front of the counter, her throat tight. She didn't sit.

"There you are, Carly," Margo said. "Where'd you go? Out on the boardwalk for a little air?"

Carly just nodded, relieved that they were too busy to notice where she had been.

"Your pizza's ready, hon. Here, Nicky'll ring it up for you." She handed the order to Nick and gave him an elbow in the side.

Nick took the box from his mother and punched the keys of the register. "Nine ninety-five," he said, staring down at the cash drawer.

Carly handed over ten one dollar bills and, without waiting for the nickel change, grabbed the pizza and soda and fled the shop, out onto the boardwalk, anonymous again amidst the throng. But the lava in her chest continued to burn and she wished with all her might that she could cry.

# CHAPTER 5

"Here you go, Eddie," Carly said, setting the pizza on her stool and dumping the change from her pocket into the bucket. "I'm going for a little walk."

"Hey," Eddie complained. "You've got to help me eat this thing. If you don't take a few pieces, I'll end up eating the whole darn pie."

"I'm not hungry anymore." Carly felt the weight of Nick's words settling into the pit of her stomach like clumps of wet sand. "You could just save me some for later, okay?"

Without waiting for an answer, Carly took off down the boardwalk, weaving in and out of the meandering families, the strolling couples, the clusters of teenagers, the senior citizens. She wandered over to a bench and watched them pass by, her chin in her hands. Hundreds of people, and she didn't fit in with any of them. Maybe that's what a dork was, a person without a place, the square peg in a room of round holes. She'd have to look up the definition when she got home. She wouldn't even be surprised if the dictionary entry included her name, e.g., Carly Chambers, Oceanside, New Jersey.

Carly felt a sharp tug on her hair. She grabbed her head and jumped to her feet.

"Surprise!"

"Aileen," Carly whined, plopping back onto the bench, "can't you just learn how to say hi like everybody else?"

"Why would I want to be like everybody else? Shove over a bit." Aileen was wearing a tiny pair of dark green shorts and an extra-large gray T-shirt. The shirt was tucked in in the front, but hung out, capelike, in the back. It was a good thing, too, because Carly was sure that those shorts were going to split when Aileen attempted to sit.

"So," Aileen began, maneuvering safely onto the bench, "when did you start hanging out on the boardwalk?"

"I don't know. Five, six weeks ago. But I'm not really hanging out."

"Not *really* hanging out? Then what are you doing up here, running away from home?"

Carly felt a familiar tightness traveling up her spine and into her neck. She stared straight ahead, her lips pressed together in a stiff, straight line.

"Personally, I never come up here unless I have to. It's so . . . so juvenile. I mean, look at these people. Don't they have a life? Alexa got a job, you know. She works in the food court in that new mini-mall over on Fisher Street. Now I'm, like, bored to death every night when she's working." Aileen paused to slurp on a red water ice, trying to scrape up the clumps that were clinging to the bottom of the cup. "Want some?" She held the water ice out toward Carly.

Carly shook her head and inched a little farther away.

Aileen threw her head back, the water ice at her mouth, and banged on the bottom of the cup. A large chunk came splashing out onto her face and dribbled down her chin and onto her shirt.

"Aaah, man!" Aileen jumped up and leaned over the boardwalk rail, shaking her head like a shaggy dog just in from the rain. When she straightened up, she was licking the droplets from around her mouth.

Carly moved to the other end of the bench, swallowing down a laugh that was curling up her throat like smoke.

Aileen started to crush the cup in her hand.

"Did you know that there's a big hunk of bubble gum stuck to the bottom of your cup?" Carly asked.

Aileen lifted the cup above her head and looked. "Oh, yeah. It's mine. I was saving it for when I was done." She pried the gum off the cup and stuck it in her mouth.

"Aileen! That is so gross. You're disgusting."

"What? It's not like I picked it up off the ground or anything."

Carly's empty stomach started flipping, and it had nothing to do with stale gum. A crowd of her classmates was walking down the boardwalk and Nick was in the middle of the pack. She felt her face beginning its slow burn and she folded her arms tightly across her chest.

"Be right back," Aileen said. "I'm all sticky. I gotta go wash this stuff off."

Carly dropped her hands in her lap and pretended to be intently studying her nails. She squeezed each finger in turn, counting, counting. By the time she got to sixty, they'd be past her. Eleven. Twelve. What would she say if they stopped? Thirteen. Nothing, of course. Just ignore them. Fourteen. Fifteen. Maybe they'd be nice, even. Sixteen. She should just get up and go, leave before they saw her. Seventeen. But maybe it would be kind of cool if they thought she was hanging out on the boardwalk. Eighteen. Nineteen. Her father had killed her social life, never allowing her to parties or school affairs. Twenty. Twenty-one. Maybe tonight she could start. Twenty-two. Show them that she wasn't a dork at all. Twenty-three. They didn't even know her!

At twenty-five, the barking started.

"Woof, woof, woof! Oh, my God, I can't control him!" Josh Manly had one of those stupid, gag dog leashes that made it look like he was walking an invisible pet.

"It's going for Carly!" he screamed, pretending to struggle with the stiff leash.

Carly flicked her eyes up into the crowd of kids that was strolling behind Josh toward the bench. They were smiling, even Nick.

Josh collapsed with feigned exhaustion when he reached Carly. "Look!" he yelled to his friends, jiggling the leash. "I was worried for nothing! Spike likes Carly."

Carly attempted a friendly smile. Should she play along and pretend to pet the invisible dog?

"Spike's a smart dog. He knows his own kind,"

someone smirked. The whole crowd cracked up.

Carly felt a hot flash rip through her chest like a bullet. But she didn't flinch. She kept her eyes focused on the board below her feet and took small, short breaths.

"C'mon, Josh," Mandy Sheperd whined, "let me walk it now. You promised."

"You can walk Carly," Josh offered.

Another burst of laughter. Carly dug her nails into the bench.

"Hey, you're in my seat. Get up." The laughter died away and everyone turned to look at Aileen.

She stood beside Josh and blew an enormous pink bubble, carefully removed it from her lips and held it out toward him. "Or else I'll have to pop this on your shrunken little head."

Josh jumped up. Aileen was odd by anybody's standards, but she was older, and older counted for a lot.

"Hey, it's all yours," Josh puffed. "This is the dork bench, anyway."

"Yeah?" Aileen popped the bubble back into her mouth. "Why don't you go look for the twit bench then. I hear it's got your name engraved on it."

Josh mumbled under his breath and the crowd moved away. Mandy made a grab for the leash and the kids all laughed again over some comment whispered too low for Carly to hear.

Aileen dropped onto the bench. "I hate this place," she sighed. She pulled a compact from her cloth purse and started dabbing some color onto her cheeks.

Her lips and two spots on her chin were still red from the water ice. "Nothing but small town twits. I'm moving to New York after I graduate. Get some acting jobs." She moved the mirror back and forth, checking out everything from her neck to the butterfly clip in her hair.

"I used to live in New York, you know, in my prior life." Aileen snapped the compact closed. "But that's a whole other story. Here, want one?" Aileen zipped open her purse and pulled out a handful of cosmetics. There must have been ten lipsticks and almost as many bottles of nail polish. "I don't even need it all. It's one of those bad habits from my New York days that I haven't gotten totally rid of. Don't tell my counselor, though." Aileen paused for a deep breath and turned on the bench to face Carly. "Speaking of New York, Carly, and I don't tell people this all the time, but I lived through some pretty bad stuff there, you know? Most of which I don't even want to think about. But I know stuff these small-town twits don't know. For instance . . . " Aileen pulled the gum from her mouth and cleared her throat.

Carly stood up and started to edge away. She had her own problems to worry about, and she sure didn't want to hang around all night listening to Aileen's life story. And that squinty-eyed, penetrating look Aileen was throwing at her made her feel creepy, like a bug under a microscope.

"You don't fool me," Aileen said. "Because I seen it before."

"I don't know what you're talking about." Carly took a few steps backward.

41

Aileen stood and followed her, closing the gap between them to inches. She took the gum from her mouth and stuck it on the back of the bench without ever looking away. "I know, Carly. I know about the stuff that goes on in your house. And you have to tell . . . "

Carly jerked away. "You don't know anything, Aileen," she hissed. "Just leave me alone."

Carly climbed over the rail that rimmed the boardwalk and dropped into the cool sand below.

"Hey! Wait!" Aileen called.

But Carly ran to the ocean's edge, the lights of the boardwalk far behind her, then sprinted up the beach in the blackness. Nick's words, her classmates' taunting, Aileen's prying were all thrashing around inside her, like sharks tangled in a fisherman's net, ripping at her. She lengthened her strides and picked up her speed. She drove herself forward in the darkness until she felt nothing but her body moving swiftly through the night. She ran until her legs ached and her throat burned with every breath, until her head was filled with nothing but the struggle for air and her heart with only the urge to run forever. Spent and gasping for breath, she finally sank to her knees in the sand.

She stared out toward the ocean and let its breeze wash over her. No matter how wickedly hot it was inland, the air always moved here, sometimes in gusts that whipped her hair around her face and sometimes as a gentle wind that touched her briefly and moved on.

On a cloudy night the darkness on the beach was almost total. You couldn't see much farther than a few feet. The ocean disappeared in the blackness, indistinguishable from the inky sky. It loomed like a sleeping giant, hidden but for the rumble of its waves and the soft fizzle of foam it left on the beach.

Carly felt the darkness wrap around her like a protective cloak, and slowly it smothered the fire that had burned so painfully in her chest.

She began to walk back along the ocean's edge. Halfway to 32nd Street, she climbed up into a wooden lifeguard stand. The stands, all identical, had a high back and sides that rose almost to her shoulder. She often sat in these stands, ten feet high, the queen of the night beach, a kingdom of darkness, and listened to the music of the rolling waves, her constant and dependable subjects.

Carly rested her chin on her knees and watched the stars. Thin clouds passed slowly in front of a half moon, giving it a slightly spooky look. Tired, she leaned back against the wooden slats and closed her eyes, lulled by the rhythm of the waves. It was only the familiar creep of fear that kept her from dozing.

She didn't have a watch and she'd lost track of how long she'd been on the beach. She'd been lucky these past few weeks, sneaking out without ever raising any suspicions. But how long could it last? How long until something went wrong?

There was a scuffling noise in the sand below her, and Carly sucked in her breath. She sat frozen, her eyes wide in the darkness. The noise stopped, then started again. Just as she leaned slightly to peek over the side

43

of the lifeguard stand, a dark figure hopped onto the front ladder and started climbing up. She hadn't seen anyone coming. He must have sneaked up on her from behind. Otherwise, she would have seen him earlier. There was no time to climb over the back. She was trapped. His head and chest popped up right in front of her. Carly gripped the sides of the stand and kicked with all her might. There was a startled scream and then a thud as the figure hit the sand below. Carly flew down the ladder and jumped over the groaning person. He wasn't moving. She bent down low to take a quick look at his face before running away.

# CHAPTER 6

"Nick!" Carly dropped to her knees beside her classmate. "Oh, my gosh!"

Nick was lying on his back in the sand staring up at her. "Carly?"

"Yeah."

"What did you do that for?" he groaned.

Carly's heart was still racing and she had to pause before she answered him. Half of her wanted to help him up, but the other half wanted to hit him again. He deserved it. She tested the harsh words she wanted to use, rolling them around inside her mouth like marbles, but she swallowed them down. "I didn't know it was you," she finally answered. "You just scared me, that's all. Can you move? Are you okay?"

Nick sat up in the sand and shook his head. "*I scared you*?"

"Well, yeah. Why didn't you say something? You just jumped up there at me. I didn't know what else to do."

"I wasn't jumping up at you! I didn't even know you were there!" Nick shouted, rubbing the back of his neck. "I didn't know anybody was there until you gave me the karate kick in the chest. Are you taking a self-protection course or something?"

Carly winced in the darkness. She certainly knew all the defensive moves, but they were self-taught. "I'll go," she said after a few moments of awkward silence. "You can have the stand. And I'm real sorry I kicked you. I didn't mean it." Carly turned and began to walk away.

"Carly!" Nick called. "Wait a minute."

She turned. She could just see him in the darkness, struggling to his feet.

"I know you didn't mean it," he said. "And, I, um, I think I'm gonna need your help."

"My help?"

"Yeah, well, I kind of twisted my ankle when I fell."

Carly finally noticed that he was leaning against the stand, his right leg bent, foot suspended just above the sand. "Oh, no," she moaned.

"It's probably nothing," Nick said quickly, "but I can't put any pressure on it right now. I think I'm just gonna try to hop back up to the boardwalk. Would you mind walking with me in case I don't make it?"

"In case you don't make it?" Pictures were flashing through Carly's mind of Nick with a casted foot telling his teammates that he couldn't pitch for the rest of the season. It was all because of Carly Chambers. Her popularity would really soar. She'd need to carry a deflector shield to school in September to survive all the withering, hateful stares she'd be getting in the halls.

"It's okay if you don't want to do it," Nick added.

"No. I mean, yes. I mean . . . sure," Carly stammered. "I'll walk with you." The last few words squeaked out of her tight throat and she kicked at the sand.

"Thanks." Nick accepted her stumbled answer as a yes and took a few tentative hops around to the back of the stand. He paused. It was a long way to the boardwalk. Carly moved just beside him in case he needed a hand to steady himself.

"Well, here goes." Nick took three lurching hops forward and then, like a clown on the high wire, tilted dangerously forward, then backward.

"Oh, no!" Carly cried. "Careful!" She reached out to help him, but he was flailing his arms for balance and accidentally hit her in the side of the face. She stumbled back, tripped on her own feet and fell in the sand. Before she could move, Nick also fell backward, crashing into her. They lay there in stunned silence for a moment, not moving, until she felt Nick's body shaking. She couldn't clearly see his face in the darkness and wondered if he was crying from the pain. But when he opened his mouth, it was laughter that spilled out, a half-giggle, half-laugh that went on and on until Carly found herself smiling without knowing why.

"Oh, man," he finally sighed, sitting up and stretching the injured ankle out in front of himself. "I guess that's not going to work."

"No," Carly agreed, shaking the sand out of her hair. "I guess not. Do you want me to go get some help?"

"Nah," Nick said. "Let me just sit here for a little bit,

see if I can't get it to loosen up some." He gingerly removed his sneaker and sock and began to rub his ankle. "Are you okay? I mean, I didn't hurt you, did I?"

Carly ran her hand down her left cheek, then covered her mouth to stop the words that wanted to come, to accuse him. He hurt her worse than he could even imagine. Part of her wanted to hurt him back. But she knew too well the strange power of cold, hard words. They started fires that killed friendships, families, and love.

"Carly?"

She pulled her hand back up to her left cheek and felt the tender spot just below her eye. "I'm okay," she answered quietly. "It's just a little bump. I guess I can't complain anyway, not after what I did to you."

"It wasn't your fault," Nick added. "I probably would've kicked you too." He stopped working on his ankle and looked up at her. "I can't believe that I picked that one stand. I mean, every other stand on the whole beach must be empty. What were you doing up there, anyway?"

Carly felt her face flush. She clutched two handfuls of sand and let the grains run through her fingers. "Just watching the ocean and thinking," she said.

"No way!" Nick blurted.

"I know it sounds weird to you because you've lived here all your life," Carly explained. "But I never saw the ocean till I came here two years ago and, I don't know how to explain it, but it's . . . it's . . . Never mind, it's too weird."

"I don't think it's weird." Nick rested his chin on his knee. "I was just surprised because that's why I was climbing up into the stand—to watch the ocean and think about stuff."

"You were?"

"Yeah. It's the best place for thinking. When I grow up, I'm gonna get a big house right on the beach with a second floor deck. Then any night I want, I'll just sleep right outside in my lounge chair next to the ocean. I think that would be so cool."

Carly drew a wide circle in the sand with her finger. "I wouldn't even mind just having a little tent right here. Every morning, I would sit outside and watch the sun come up. My favorite part is when the first bit of light starts creeping across the horizon, like a purple glow, and the darkness starts thinning out ever so slightly. The whole world seems to be slowly, magically appearing out of nothingness, you know? And then, when the sun comes and the colors run up the sky, the pinks and the oranges . . . " Carly suddenly fell silent. She must sound like an idiot. The darkness thins out ever so slightly. Did she actually say that? Here she is going on and on about sunrises like she was some kind of expert. She had only watched the sun come up over the beach once. It had been so beautiful, but much too dangerous to try again. Her parents were awake when she got back. She was no sooner in her room than her father was yelling for her to hurry up and get downstairs. He had another errand for her to run, and he didn't like to be kept waiting. It frightened her all day to think that if she had dawdled only five minutes more on the beach, he might have discovered her secret. She never went to see the sunrise again.

Carly turned to find Nick staring at her, his chin off his knees, his mouth open. She felt her face burning and she hoped that it wasn't glowing in the dark.

"I never heard you talk that much before," he said.

Carly jumped to her feet. "Yeah, well, I guess I slipped up. I better get going."

Nick didn't move. "Do you like to write?"

Carly shrugged. She did, but it was too dangerous. She couldn't keep things like that around her house.

"Because I do," Nick continued. "I like to write stuff just like the way you were talking, images and things. But I don't know anybody else who does. Help me up, okay?"

Carly held out her hand and Nick took it, pulling himself up. He stood unsteadily beside her and stared down at the sand. Carly thought he was testing the strength of the ankle, weighing his chances.

"How's it feel?" she asked.

Nick looked up at her. "Listen, Carly," he began. "About that stuff on the boardwalk earlier tonight? I'm sorry, you know? I didn't know Josh was going to be such a jerk. I'm not like that."

Carly felt the fire rekindling, heard the echo of their laughter as they left her. "Sure," she mumbled. "Should we try for the boardwalk again?"

"Yeah. Let's do it."

Nick limped to the boardwalk, saying little, concentrating

on his steps and holding Carly's hand for balance. His hand was smooth and firm, and she felt the pressure of his grip with each small hop he took. For a little while, she let herself pretend that he wasn't hurt, that they were holding hands like the couples she saw in the halls at school or on the boardwalk at night.

They finally made it to the boardwalk, and Nick hopped up the first three steps and sat on the fourth. Carly stood in the sand, just out of the lights. "You okay?" she asked.

"Yeah," Nick said, but he was breathing hard. "It's not too bad. I was wondering, you know . . . um . . . tomorrow . . . "

"Hey, Nick!"

Josh Manly and the crowd of Nick's friends were walking up the boardwalk, coming toward them. "Where you been?" someone yelled.

Nick looked quickly from his approaching friends to Carly. She saw the fear in his eyes, which were big as baseballs.

"Who you with? Who's that down there?" It was Kevin Chandler, Nick's right fielder.

Carly backed up farther into the darkness. That was the great advantage of the night beach. It was easy to disappear. She turned and ran, giving Nick the freedom to make up an identity for her, to spare him the embarrassment of being caught on the beach with one of the most unpopular kids in the school. He was just as bad as the rest of them. Who needed him, anyway?

Carly ducked under the boardwalk and came up on

the other side, about half a block from where she left Nick. He was surrounded by his friends, the whole crowd slowly moving him toward Margo's. She could only see the back of his head, bent low, as though he were survey-ing his ankle. She wondered how well he lied.

She turned her back on him and headed toward the newspaper stand. From a clock in the jewelry story window, she saw that it was late. She could only make a quick stop to see Eddie before heading home.

"Hey, Eddie," Carly said, leaning on the ledge of his window opening.

"There you are!" he exclaimed, fanning himself with an old magazine.

The stacks of newspapers were growing short. Two pieces of cold pepperoni pizza were sitting in the box on her stool.

"I saved 'em for you," Eddie said. "Just like I prom-ised, even though they've been calling my name for the last hour."

Carly smiled. She pulled the two pieces apart and handed one to Eddie. "I just want one," she said, "'cause I gotta get going."

"Hey," Eddie said. "Remember the basketball player from earlier tonight?"

"What?"

"You know, the one who didn't get his contract renewed and became a musician?"

"Oh, yeah," Carly said. "That basketball player."

"Well," Eddie continued, leaning toward her, "he came back. And the only news he was looking for was news about you."

"About me?" Carly felt a sudden chill and her throat closed up around the piece of pizza she had just swallowed.

"Are you in some kind of trouble, honey?"

"I don't know. I don't know," Carly said. "I better go home."

"I didn't tell him anything, Carly. Heck, I don't really know anything to tell except that I know you're a good kid. He's got an official lookin' badge, though. And he's hanging around. Don't turn too quick like, but he's sitting over there on the bench, across from Rita's Water Ice."

Carly turned her head very slightly and glanced at the man out of the corner of her eye. He was looking straight at her. "I gotta go, Eddie." And she raced home as fast as she could.

# CHAPTER 7

"I'm coming! I'm coming!" Carly yelled, jumping out of bed at the sound of her father's voice.

"You have one minute and then I'm coming up there," he boomed. "And by God, I'll know how to wake you up."

Carly glanced at the clock—7:30. She had slept only fitfully last night, jumping up frequently at every noise, peering out the window for any sign of the stranger from the boardwalk. She had never undressed, and now she had no time to change into a new outfit. She did a quick check in the mirror to make sure there were no telltale pizza or soda stains on her clothes. She threw her hair into a ponytail. The wind had made it a mass of tangles and there was no time to brush them all out.

Carly opened her door and descended slowly to the kitchen on the second floor, tightly gripping the rail. If the man on the boardwalk knew her father, she was dead. They didn't have truant officers in the summer, as far as she knew. And she wasn't out past the town's curfew hour for minors. She couldn't figure out why an officer would be asking questions about her.

Mr. Chambers was sitting at the table drinking coffee and eating a plate of bacon and scrambled eggs. The small kitchen was filled with the smell of his breakfast. "Well, well, princess. Were you planning on sleeping all day?"

Carly took one quick glance at his face but saw nothing new there. Either he didn't know about her trips to the boardwalk, or he was hiding it very well. She went to stand beside her mother, who was at the stove with the frying pan.

"Did you oversleep?" Mrs. Chambers asked quietly.

"Yeah, I did." Carly fingered the hot pad, twisting it around on the counter.

Mr. Chambers bit into a piece of toast, his eye on Carly. "The least you could do, Leila, is teach your daughter some personal hygiene. Look at her."

Mrs. Chambers emptied the grease from the pan into a small cup, her unsteady hand spilling some on the counter. "Did you fall asleep in your clothes, honey?"

"Yes." Carly plucked a piece of crisp bacon from the serving plate on the counter. "I was reading late and I fell asleep with the book."

"I used to do that all the time," her mother said, wiping up the pool of grease with a paper towel. "There's nothing better than to fall asleep with a good book. I remember . . . "

"Where's the rest of that bacon?" Mr. Chambers interrupted, scooping the last bit of egg into his mouth. "I've got work to do."

"Carly, why don't you run up and change?" Mrs. Chambers suggested, scraping the bacon onto her husband's plate.

"She doesn't have time, Leila," he said. "I've got errands for her to run."

"Okay, then, Carly." Her mother pulled a plate from the cupboard. "Sit right down and eat so you can go."

Mr. Chambers banged his coffee mug on the table and turned slowly in his chair. "I said, she doesn't have time."

"But, Vinnie, she didn't even have dinner last night and . . ."

He pointed his fork at her, eyes narrowed, jaw set, and she fell silent. "If she wanted to have breakfast, she should have gotten herself out of bed." He turned to Carly. "Two packages. They're down in the store on the counter. Here are the addresses. Don't leave them on the porch or with anybody except for these two men right here." He shook the paper in front of her face. "Got it?"

Carly snatched the paper from his hand and turned to leave.

"And Carly," he added, his voice low and threatening, "if you mess this up, you'll be very sorry." He set the timer to sixty minutes, and placed it in the center of the kitchen table. "You'd better be here when this goes off."

Carly took a quick glance at the clock and left the kitchen. She found the two packages, heavy candy boxes wrapped in brown paper and tied with string. She dropped them in a small backpack she kept behind the counter.

"Carly! Wait." Her mother came swiftly down the hall into the shop in her bedroom slippers. "Here." She slipped a muffin in Carly's hand and looked back over her shoulder. "Do you know where you're going? Will you be okay?"

Carly looked down at the paper in her hand. "Yeah. I'll be fine." She had been to both of these addresses many times before.

"Be careful," her mother warned. "Things have been . . . " Mrs. Chambers grimaced, searching for the right word. She squeezed Carly's hand.

The timer upstairs was ticking away. "I'll be fine," Carly insisted and pulled herself free of her mother's grasp.

The clouds from last night had thinned out and the sun was brilliant and warm. It would get soupy and hazy later in the day, but this early in the morning everything was fresh and sharp.

Carly chewed on her blueberry muffin while she walked and watched the people around her. She could always tell the newcomers from those who had been in town for a week or two. The new arrivals had red skin and funny white lines on their backs from yesterday's bathing suit. Many of the town's full-time residents derisively called these vacationers "shoobies" and looked forward to the first cool winds of September to drive them all back home. But Carly hated the way the town changed when they left. Like a tree whose leaves suddenly drooped and fell, Oceanside lost all its color and form and life.

Her muffin gone, Carly decided to run to each of her deliveries. If there were any time left over, she would use every bit of it and enjoy a leisurely walk back. Her first stop was on Bay Avenue near 28th Street. It was one of the older and less attractive areas in Oceanside. Carly decided to take Jamison Street. It would take her through to 28th, it had sidewalks and there was much less traffic than on Bay. She wore her sneakers today and easily sprinted block after block, the blueberry muffin gurgling around in her otherwise empty stomach.

She hopped up the steps onto the porch of the first house and unzipped her backpack. The door swung open before she could ring the bell.

"Come in. Come in," said the man, sticking his head out the door and glancing up and down the street.

Carly hesitated. She usually just handed him his package and left. She didn't want to waste any time. But he put his arm around her shoulder and guided her into the house.

"Thank you," he said, taking the package from her. His living room was dim and disorganized. There was a black-and-white movie playing on the small television. He was an older man, slightly stooped, with thick, well-combed white hair. He had a nervous habit that she had noticed on other deliveries, blinking his eyes every second or two. Now they were fluttering so rapidly that she wondered how he was even able to see.

"You're panting," he said. "Was someone chasing you?"

"No." Carly took a deep breath to settle her breathing. The air in the room was stale and close. "I just like to run."

"You're sure?" He tried to hold his eyes wide open.

"Yes, I'm sure," she said, backing toward the door.

He eyed her up and down, then reached into his pocket and pulled out a five dollar bill. He pushed it into her hand. "This is for your trouble."

"Oh, no," Carly protested, holding the money out toward him. "I couldn't. My father said . . . well . . . he'd . . . "

The man shook his head. "I bet he would too. Your father's a . . . " He paused, and the blinking began again in earnest. He rubbed his hand over his whiskered face. "Well, anyway, this'll just be our little secret."

Carly didn't want to be here, to share any secrets with this man. She dropped the bill on the nearest chair and bolted for the door. "I gotta go," she said.

"No, wait. Please. Can't we talk for a minute? I just wanted to ask you. . . "

He made a move toward her, and Carly pushed her way out the door, sprinting up the street and around the corner. She shivered, shaking off the touch of that odd man and the smell of his damp house.

The next delivery was about ten blocks away. She was making good time. She backtracked along Jamison toward 36th Street. She ran five blocks, then paused at the corner of 33rd Avenue to wait for the light. There was no one else on the street. She tilted her head back and held her arms out to the sky. She felt like it was raining sun, a downpour of sweet yellow warmth, soaking into her face, her hair, and her clothes. She wished she could make deliveries all day, watching the sun float across the sky and the crowds drift to and from the beach.

"Are you worshiping a sun god or something?"

Carly dropped her arms and whirled around. Aileen was sitting on a bench in the shade, up against Koller's Bakery, chewing on a powdered jelly doughnut.

"Don't you ever stay home?" Carly asked.

"I could ask you the same question," Aileen retorted. "Want one?" Aileen held the white bakery bag out toward Carly.

The traffic light turned green. Carly hesitated. She was hungry, and doughnuts were very hard to resist. She had made good time so far. She probably had enough time for one. "Okay. Thanks." Carly plopped beside Aileen on the bench and looked in the bag. Chocolate cream was her favorite, but it could be messy. She opted for the glazed. She took a huge first bite. The doughnut was soft and fresh and still faintly warm, and she savored the sensation of all that sugary sweetness melting in her mouth. "This is *so* good," she mumbled.

Aileen smiled. She was wearing a bikini top and a long flowing skirt. "Yeah. I went in to apply for a job, but I couldn't resist buying the doughnuts."

"Did you get it?"

Aileen licked the white powder from her fingers. "The job? Nope."

"You don't exactly look like a baker, anyway." Carly pushed the last piece of doughnut in her mouth.

"Yeah. Can you see me in one of those goofy white hats?"

Carly laughed. "I doubt they even make them in your size." Aileen's hair was springier than ever, rising ever higher with the humidity.

Aileen sighed. "I don't even want a job, anyway. It's just that Alexa's working all the time now, and she's got money and I don't. I can't sponge off her forever."

"Why don't you work at the bed-and-breakfast?"

Aileen snorted. "Sure. I'll carry the silver serving tray in for the afternoon tea. Are you kidding? Harry and Sandra would have to be completely paralyzed before they'd let me do anything in that freaky museum."

Aileen's parents ran a Victorian bed-and-breakfast that looked like a large-scale dollhouse. From the porch to the garden to the white picket fence, it was perfect. The only thing that ever appeared out of place there was Aileen.

"So, where'd you get that bruise on your cheek?"

Carly put her hand to her face and felt a small lump where Nick had accidentally hit her. She didn't know that it was showing. "Not where you think," she answered.

"Has your father always been that way?"

Carly turned on the bench. Aileen sat slouched, examining her long, orange nails, red hair fringing her face and a white ring of powdered sugar around her lips. She looked comical, like a clown.

Carly couldn't help smiling. She slumped down next to Aileen. Maybe it was the sugar coursing through her veins and the sweet taste in her mouth. Or maybe it was because she was tired and spent and everything seemed so unreal, relaxing on this bench on a beautiful morning, Aileen stretched out beside her like an escapee from the circus. It slipped out before she had time to consider the consequences. "Yeah," Carly admitted. "He has."

Carly reached back to her earliest memories. It's not that there weren't any good things in her childhood. But the bad memories were somehow greater, heavier, suffocating any happy times she had had. Like when she was six and he walked her to school on the opening day of first grade. She remembered the feel of his strong hand in hers, how happy she was that he wanted to walk with her. He told her how much smarter she would be than all the other kids, how he wanted her to do well and make him proud.

She was so excited learning her first words, reading her first book. At night, she would sit at the dinner table, legs swinging, too short to reach the floor, and try to tell her parents about the new games the class played or her favorite story in the reader. She always began well, but then she would notice how intently her father was staring at her. She would become nervous, and her sentences became twisted and her thoughts all tangled up. He would reach across the table and smack her on the side of the head again and again "to get the cobwebs out," until her ears rang. She learned quickly to keep her stories to herself.

"You okay?" Aileen asked quietly.

Carly lifted her head from the back of the bench. "I'm fine. But I gotta go. It's getting late."

Aileen sat up as well. "It is not late. It's early morning. Just sit back and relax for half an hour."

"You don't understand," Carly sighed. "He has me on a timer. I have to be back before it goes off or else."

"Or else what?"

Things were going too far. It was stupid to have said anything to Aileen. Carly stood and grabbed her backpack. "I gotta go."

"You should tell somebody," Aileen advised. "I'm not kidding."

"There's nothing to tell." Carly walked to the corner and waited for the light to change.

"It'll only get worse!" Aileen called after her. "Believe me. I know!"

The light turned green, and Carly began to cross the street. A tall man came out of Brynn's Bagels, absorbed in his newspaper, and a woman rounded the corner, bumping a baby stroller over the uneven pavement. The woman must have asked him for the time, because he lowered the paper slightly and looked at his watch. Carly froze in the middle of the street. It was the man from the boardwalk! He tucked the paper under his arm and started toward her. He smiled and put one hand in the air, trying to flag her down as though she were a taxi.

Carly turned back and saw Aileen, arms crossed, watching them both. Heat was rising off the street and shimmered, in waves, between them. The light turned red and traffic began to move toward her.

"Don't you say a word to him," Carly called quickly

to Aileen, "or I'll tell about all those lipsticks in your purse! I swear I will." Then Carly ran, not bothering with the sidewalks, but running with the cars, darting between lanes and finally, at 39th Street, slipping down a small alley. There was a blue pickup truck parked beside an overgrown bush, and she dropped on the ground between them. She gripped the straps of her backpack, breathing heavily, and carefully watched both ends of the alley. But the man didn't appear. A dog two houses away came out on its porch and began to bark wildly at her. She got slowly to her feet and peered over the edge of the truck bed. No tall man in sight. She left the alley and, still not seeing him, sprinted to her next delivery. She handed the package through the door without a word to a young bearded man and ran straight home. She beat the timer by five minutes. It was sitting on the counter in the shop.

Her father came out of the back office. "You're sweating," he said.

He was too, but she didn't mention it. "It's hot," she answered. She scoured his face, his body movements, for some knowledge of the tall man, but there was nothing. Her father always had a certain swagger about him whenever he trapped her in some crime or discovered a secret. But he was standing perfectly still, arms crossed, no color rising in his face, no clench in his hands.

"Any trouble?" he asked.

She shook her head.

"No problems, then?"

Carly looked him straight in the eyes. "No problems," she lied.

"Good," he said with a big sigh, patting her on the back. "Good job. Why don't you run up to the kitchen, then, and get something to eat. Take a little break." He picked up the timer and turned the face until it dinged and the ticking stopped.

It wasn't often that she did everything right and even less often that he complimented her. Carly sat at the small glass-topped table in the kitchen and poured herself a bowl of Cheerios. She half-wished that he would keep his nice thoughts to himself. Just when she was hating him the most, he would do something kind out of the blue, like compliment her hair or buy her a Beanie Baby. It was like trudging through a garbage dump and coming across a small patch of rare endangered flowers. Just when you were ready to condemn the whole place, you couldn't, because it sheltered something worthwhile.

Two things, however, were certain. Her father didn't know anything about the tall man. And she wasn't going to tell him.

# CHAPTER 8

Carly sat on the stool outside the newsstand, the bucket on her lap, and ran her fingers through the coins. Eddie was doing a brisk business.

"Dog groomer," he said, nodding at his last customer.

"No way!" Carly laughed. "He was a jet fighter pilot."

Eddie pulled a checkered handkerchief from his shirt pocket. "I was going to be a jet fighter pilot when I was younger," he reminisced, wiping his face and the back of his neck.

"You were?"

"Yep. There was just one little thing that held me back."

"What was that?" Carly asked.

"The seats were too small." Eddie burst out laughing, his oversized stomach bouncing around beneath the apron and his facing turning red. He always enjoyed his own jokes.

She had been sitting here with him for at least half an hour and he hadn't asked her one question about the strange man from last night. That's the way he was. She could come to the stand one night wearing a big dead fish on the top of her head, and he wouldn't say a word about it. He respected her privacy. He always waited until she was ready to talk.

And she was. She didn't know what to do about this guy who was spying on her. It was very creepy, like lying in the dark worrying about the huge spider you failed to catch. Was it under the bureau on the other side of the room or on the ceiling just above your head, ready to drop?

"Eddie," Carly asked, "you know that tall guy from last night?"

"Yeah?"

"What exactly did he want to know about me?"

Eddie was emptying the change from his apron and dropping it in the bucket. "Like I said yesterday," he began, "I didn't tell him much because I don't know much. He wanted to know about your family, how often you come up here on the boardwalk. Stuff like that. He wanted to know if you worked for me or if you were selling anything up here."

"Selling anything?"

Eddie gave her a quick sidelong glance. "Yeah. Like drugs. That kind of stuff."

"Drugs! Eddie, I swear I don't sell drugs."

"I didn't think you did."

"But why's he following me? Why would he think I sell drugs?" Carly dug her hand into the bucket and squeezed a fistful of coins.

67

Eddie shook his head. "Hey. It was just one night. Maybe he was checking out a false tip. You checked out okay. Case closed. You probably won't see any more of him."

Carly released the coins and leaned forward on the bucket, lowering her voice. "But I did see him again, Eddie. He followed me today too."

"Uh oh." Eddie whistled and crossed his arms against his chest. "That's not good. Did you tell your parents?"

Carly sat quietly for a moment looking at the ground. Except for that little slip with Aileen today, she never talked about her family, not to the teachers or guidance counselors or even the few classmates who had asked.

She knew Eddie wasn't going to blab about her life to anyone, but it was still way too embarrassing. Even though she thought of him as a friend, she didn't want him to peek into her closet, to see the mess of her life that was hidden there behind the door.

Several customers lined up at the stand and Carly went back to sorting the coins without answering his question. The last of the customers was a father trying to buy a newspaper. The baby in his arms was lunging at every paper and magazine within reach, and the toddler at his feet kept trying to run away. Every time the man stooped to retrieve a thrown magazine, the baby would reach out and grab another from the rack and toss it to the ground. The toddler ran around the stool and peeked in the door of the stand. Eddie invited her in, then pulled her up onto his knee. "Here you go," Eddie said. "Do you want to sell Daddy the newspaper?"

The little girl banged her hands on the counter and let out a loud, giggling scream. The father finally got his paper and headed off, a child in each arm. Carly picked up the few scattered magazines.

"She was a cutie, wasn't she?" Eddie smiled. "I love 'em at that age, all innocent and funny."

"Yeah. She was cute. And brave too."

"Brave?"

"Well, she wasn't afraid of you."

"No kids are afraid of me! They love me!"

Carly smiled.

"It's true. I even play Santa Claus at the Christmas Bazaar at Holy Innocents Church every year."

Carly stuffed *Newsweek* down into the rack. Eddie would make a good Santa Claus, and not just because of his oversized belly. She looked at his smiling eyes, his large hands smoothing down the papers. "Do you have any kids?" she asked.

Eddie dropped his eyes to his lap and stuck his hands in his apron pockets. "Yeah," he answered, not looking up. "I got a boy."

"How old?"

"Just turned thirteen last month."

Carly was sorry now that she had asked. Eddie looked out toward the ocean. His face, full of laughter a moment ago, now sagged, like a happy face balloon losing air.

"I bet he's a great kid," Carly offered.

"He's okay," Eddie said. "He's going through some stuff, but he'll be okay."

"Does he ever help you out up here?" Carly asked.

Eddie took a long sip from the straw in his soft drink. "My son doesn't know about me, Carly."

The wind was whipping in off the ocean, lifting candy wrappers high in the air and swirling the sand and dirt on the boardwalk into little piles. Carly thought that maybe she didn't hear him right. "What?" she asked, moving the stool closer to the stand.

Eddie put a rock on the top of the newspaper stack. The uppermost edges of the paper were rippling up and down, snapping at the wind like a leashed dog. "It's better he doesn't know me," Eddie said.

"No way!" Carly blurted. "That's not true. How can you say that?" She'd take Eddie as her father in a minute.

"You don't understand, Carly. His mom remarried before he was even born. He's got another dad."

"But, Eddie . . . !"

"Listen, Carly, I'm starving here. Would you run to Margo's and get me an Italian hoagie?" He pulled a stack of ones from his apron pocket and held them out toward her.

"Okay," she said slowly, taking the bills from his hand.

"And get yourself something," Eddie called after her. "You're way too skinny."

The wind was snapping at the store awnings and overturning outdoor displays. Carly drew her ponytail over her shoulder and pulled her hands through it as she walked, twisting the ends around her fingers. She hoped Nick wasn't going to be there. Every time she thought about him her stomach started surfing. She considered getting the Italian hoagie at some other shop, but Eddie would know the difference right away.

Carly ducked into a T-shirt shop a few stores up from Margo's. She needed time to think. She flipped through a rack of shirts, mindlessly, trying to figure out what she would say if she ran into Nick. Drop dead. Get lost. Just leave me alone, okay? I don't need this. Carly shoved through the smalls and started on the mediums, squeaking each hanger forcefully along the metal rack. Don't worry, I won't tell anyone that you actually spoke to me. Your reputation is safe. But what if his foot is broken and he's standing there in a cast? She stopped midway through the larges, gripping a green T-shirt. She'd say she was sorry, then ignore him, get out of the pizza shop as quickly as possible.

There was a sharp tug on the back of her shirt that almost choked her. Carly spun around.

"Shopping for new threads?" Frankie spread his arms across the aisle and rested each hand on a rack of shirts. Justin stood behind him snickering.

Carly was in the back corner of the store, rows of different colored tops hanging all around her. She looked over her shoulder. There was nowhere to go.

"Don't worry, we'll help," Frankie offered. "Won't we, Justin?"

They started pulling some of the more obnoxious

shirts from the racks, ones that made Carly cringe when she saw people wearing them. He took them off the hangers and threw them at her. "Here's a good one for you," he snorted, reading the crude sayings. "Here's another one. Hey, Justin. I know the perfect shirt for Carly. See if you can find any with a picture of a big, fat, disgusting old guy on it. That's what Carly likes, don't you, Carly?"

Frankie had a wad of keys clipped to the front belt loop of his jeans. Carly always wondered why he carried them around, how many doors could he possibly have access to. It was like he owned the boardwalk and had a key to every shop and store.

"Hey, Carly. Got any money?" Frankie asked.

She turned her back to him and pretended to be absorbed in the folded gray shirts on the shelf.

"I'll bet she does," Justin said.

"Hand it over, Carly." Frankie took a step closer to her. She heard the keys jangling and she whirled to face him. "Don't worry, fat man will give you more. Give it here."

Carly crossed her arms and stared at him, but said nothing. Eddie had told her that when she got into a situation like this with Frankie, she should scream. Just like the 911 call, he said, Frankie would panic and run away. But she just couldn't do it. Her screams were as dried up as her tears, and she couldn't even imagine such a sound escaping from her lips. Besides, other than a few shoves and trips, Frankie had never actually attacked her. He wasn't much bigger than she was and she would hit him back.

"Give it up, Carly, or else I'll come and take it."

The money was in her back pocket and, without thinking, Carly slid her hand over it. Frankie lunged forward and grabbed her arms and Justin came around from behind to lift the money from her pocket.

"Give it back!" Carly snatched at the bills that Frankie was now dangling in the air.

"Hey! What are you kids doing back there!" An older woman wearing an "I'm The Boss" T-shirt was stomping toward the back of the store.

Frankie and Justin, howling with laughter, dashed past her out of the store. Carly had to give them a head start.

"Oh, God!" the woman moaned, catching sight of the shirts strewn on the floor.

Carly tried to run, but the woman grabbed her by the ponytail. "You're going to clean this up. I'm calling the cops. I am so sick of you kids."

Carly was shaking. She couldn't have anything to do with the cops. What if they tried to take her home or called her parents? Using both hands she yanked the ponytail with all her might. Her eyes stung and her scalp burned with a thousand needlelike pricks, but she was free. She ran from the store, the woman calling after her and waving the handful of hair that was left in her grasp. Carly ducked into Margo's, still shaking, and moved all the way in to the end of the counter. She dropped her head into her hands. She forgot. She couldn't get Eddie his hoagie now because she had no money.

"What's up, Carly?" Margo leaned down, elbows on

the counter and touched Carly's shoulder. "You okay?"

Carly lifted her head and nodded. The wind was blowing in the small restaurant, lifting napkins from the tables, snatching steam from hot pizzas and carrying it out of sight.

"Eddie up for another pizza tonight?" Margo scooped some money off the counter and tossed a handful of dirty silverware into a gray bin.

"No," Carly answered, standing. "He wants an Italian hoagie, but I forgot the money. I'll have to come back."

"Don't be silly. You sit right down. Eddie's good for the money. You can bring it back anytime. Go on over and sit in the back booth. I'll bring you a piece of pizza."

"But . . ."

"Go, go, sit," Margo commanded, turning to open the oven door.

Carly shuffled to the back booth, her eyes on the ground. She was about to slide into the seat when she saw that it was occupied and jumped back.

"Hey, Carly," Nick greeted her. "Sit down." He had his back to the wall and his right leg was stretched out on the bench seat. There were lots of papers spread out on the table.

Carly glanced back at the counter stool. A customer had just slipped into her place. She looked down at Nick and slowly sat across from him, all her planned conversation instantly draining from her head, like soda from a punctured cup.

Nick punched a few numbers on his calculator and wrote the figures down on the paper in front of him.

Carly stared at her hands, twisting them in her lap.

"How's your . . . you know . . . your ankle," Carly stumbled, glancing across the table at his propped foot. At least he wasn't wearing a cast.

"The doctor said I just twisted it. There's no swelling or anything. I'm just supposed to keep off it until it feels okay." Nick leaned across the table. "It feels pretty good," he whispered, "but don't let my mom or Angela know."

Angela was Nick's older sister and seemed to have the same nervous energy as her mother. She was rushing from table to table, taking orders, serving pizza, scribbling checks, her dark hair tied up loosely in a bun. She grabbed a tray and came toward them.

"How ya doing, bud?" Angela asked, sliding some papers out of the way and putting two slices of pizza in front of Carly.

"Ah, it's killing me, Angela. I can hardly move it. You wouldn't mind getting me a Coke, would ya?"

"Poor baby." Angela looked at Carly and rolled her eyes. "Don't you worry, Carly," she said. "Nicky's always been the fragile one in the family. It wasn't your fault." Angela leaned down and whispered in Carly's ear. "I wish I could have seen it!"

Carly felt her face flush. Nick must have told her about the kick. Angela darted off to serve a customer and returned in a minute with two Cokes. She was tall and athletic and moved through the small, crowded shop like Michael Jordan through a pack of defenders. She placed the cups on the table and wiped her hands on her checkered apron. "Take care of him, Carly," she teased, winking and slipping off to clear another table.

"Isn't she great?" Nick asked.

Carly nodded, watching Angela joke with a customer, her hands always in motion, sweeping crumbs from the table, refilling the napkin dispenser, wiping down the salt shaker.

"She knows I'm faking, but she's letting me get away with it. I get to sit here doing the paperwork instead of standing behind the counter all night."

Carly pulled the wrapper off her straw and began to play with it, folding it into an accordion then twisting it around her finger into a spiral. She didn't want to sit there like a mute, but her throat was tight, squeezing off the words she thought she should say. He wouldn't be sitting here with her if any of his friends were around, and she wanted to nail him for that, let him know what a hypocrite he was. She stared down at her pizza, teeth clenched.

"Something wrong with the pizza?" Nick asked.

"No, nothing's wrong with the *pizza*," Carly growled. "The *pizza's* the best. I'm just not real hungry right now." She had lost her appetite in the T-shirt shop along with Eddie's money.

"You better eat it," Nick suggested. "My mom gets her feelings hurt when people don't eat her food. It's a wonder I don't weigh two hundred pounds."

Carly fingered the edge of her paper plate. Not only was she not hungry, she didn't want to eat across from Nick with him watching her every bite. What if she got a piece of warm cheese stuck between her front teeth or dribbled tomato sauce down her chin? Carly carefully pulled the two slices apart. "How about if you eat one?" she suggested, sliding the plate across the table.

"Sure. Why not?" Nick folded the slice in half, like a sandwich, and took a huge bite.

Angela glided up to the booth with a white paper bag. "Here's Eddie's hoagie, Carly. Nicky! You're not supposed to eat Carly's pizza! You pig!"

Nick tried to defend himself, but his mouth was so full of food that they couldn't understand a word he said.

"I asked him to eat one," Carly offered.

"He is such a weasel sometimes," Angela sighed. "I'll get you another piece."

"No, no. It's okay. I have to go." Carly jumped up and grabbed the bag. "Eddie's waiting for me."

"Carly! You eat that pizza, honey," Margo called from behind the counter. "You're all skin and bones. Heaven knows, Eddie's got enough reserves that he can wait for you. Eat up."

"I'll just take it with me." Carly picked up the pizza and started for the exit.

"Carly, wait!" Margo called. "Nicky's going with you."

"I am?"

"Yes. You carry that bag so the poor thing can eat her pizza."

"But . . . "

"If you nurse that ankle much longer, boy, it'll atrophy. Get going."

"I'm going. I'm going." Nick slid out of the booth

and limped up the aisle, dragging his leg and moaning in mock agony.

Carly stood at the front of the shop, the sharp wind tugging at her clothes and whipping her hair about her face. She'd outrun Nick and save him the embarrassment. She didn't need anyone to walk with her anyway. She looked out across the boardwalk and froze. A chill ran up her spine and she felt the tingle of hair rising on the back of her neck.

"Ready?" Nick asked, jingling the change in his pocket.

Carly didn't answer or look at him. She was transfixed, staring out across the boardwalk.

"Hey, I was only kidding," Nick said, waving his hand in front of her face as though she were a zombie. "Look. It doesn't even hurt anymore." He began to jump up and down in front of her. "Ouch! All right. Maybe I shouldn't jump yet, but I can walk fine."

"I can't leave," Carly mumbled, still staring.

On the other side of the boardwalk, leaning up against the rail and staring directly at her, was the tall man.

# CHAPTER 9

"What? What do you mean you can't leave?" Nick moved in front of Carly, blocking her view.

"I'm hungry. I think I'll eat my pizza first." Carly turned abruptly and hurried to the booth at the back of the shop. She threw the pizza on the table and slid all the way across the seat to the wall.

Nick stalked down the aisle, his limp suddenly gone, and stopped beside the table, glaring at Carly. She lifted the pizza to her mouth, but then dropped it back on the plate without taking a bite. There was no way she could eat. She met Nick's eyes.

"So eat," he commanded, all humor gone from his voice.

Carly looked down at the cold slice of pizza. "I'm not hungry anymore."

"But two seconds ago you said . . . " Nick dropped into the seat across from her. He folded his arms on the table and leaned toward her. "Carly, what's going on?"

She was playing with the pizza crust, ripping off little pieces and rolling them up into balls. She didn't know what to do. She'd probably be better off making a run for it. If the tall man decided to follow her into the pizza shop, she'd be trapped. And then there was Nick. He was staring at her with his small, chocolate eyes, eyebrows raised.

Carly jumped up. "I better go."

"Fine. Leave." Nick slumped back in the booth and pulled his cap low over his face. "But if you didn't want me to walk back with you, you should've just said so. If you're trying to get me back for that stuff that happened on the boardwalk last night, congratulations. You're doin' a great job."

"Nick, it's not that . . . " Carly twisted her hands. It's true that she had wanted to hurt him last night, to pay him back, but this didn't feel right.

"It's not like I care or anything." Nick took off his cap and flung it on the table. "I'm not exactly thrilled about being seen with you on the boardwalk, anyway."

Carly's shoulders dropped. "Yeah, that was pretty obvious."

"Why don't you just go, then?" Nick fumed. "Or are you going to stand there all night?"

"Nick, listen, this doesn't have anything to do with you. I mean, I wanted to walk...I can't...It's just that..." She knew she sounded like an idiot and was just making things worse. But she didn't want to leave it this way. She didn't want to see that cold look of indifference on his face every time she came in for Eddie's dinner. Nick kept his head down, refusing to look at her. She dropped back into the seat and leaned toward him.

"Nick," she blurted, "somebody's following me!"

"What?" He sat up.

"Some tall man. Everywhere I go. He was asking Eddie a bunch of questions about me last night. He's outside right now, leaning against the rail. That's why I can't leave."

"Where?" Nick twisted in his seat to peer out onto the boardwalk.

"Don't turn around!" Carly hissed at him, gripping the edge of the table.

"But why's he following *you*?" Nick's small eyes had grown wide.

"I don't know," Carly moaned.

Angela glided up to the table, a large round pizza tray in her hand. "Nicky, are you driving this poor girl to distraction?" She turned to Carly. "What in the world happened to your pizza?"

Carly looked at her plate. The slice was mutilated, the crust torn from the pizza and ripped into dozens of little pieces.

"Sit down." Nick grabbed Angela's arm and pulled her into the booth.

"What's going on, you two?" The tray was still suspended in her left hand.

"Some guy's following Carly," Nick said quietly. "We gotta get her out of here."

"Where is he?" Angela demanded, dropping the tray on the table and turning in her seat.

"Don't look!" Carly and Nick yelled in unison.

"Why not?" Angela asked. "You tell me which one he is.

I'll call the cops and point him out."

"No!" Carly insisted, hugging her arms to her body. She lowered her voice. "He is the police. He's got a badge. Eddie said so."

"Honey," Angela intoned, leaning across the table, "any creep can get a phony badge. Besides, why would the police be following you? Are you in some kind of trouble?"

"I don't think so," Carly said slowly, "but I don't want you to call the police. Please. I'm just going to make a run for it."

Carly started to stand, but Angela reached across the table and pushed her back down. "No, you're not."

"Please, I gotta go," Carly begged.

"Look at me," Angela demanded. "You promise me you're not involved in anything bad?"

"I promise. I promise." Carly slid to the edge of the booth. She couldn't let Angela call the police. She'd fight her way out of the shop if she had to.

"Okay, then." Angela grabbed Carly's wrist. "There's a back exit, down the hall past the bathrooms. Nicky'll go with you, won't you Nick?"

Nick nodded.

"Run straight home and tell your parents. You can't fool around with this kind of creep. Got it?"

"Hey, Angela!" Margo yelled from behind the counter. "What's going on over there, a convention?"

The wind lifted a stray napkin and it twisted strangely in the air, like a wounded bird, and fell at Carly's feet. She pulled at Angela's hold on her wrist and shook her head very slightly. "Please don't," Carly mouthed. It was bad enough that Angela was involved. She didn't want Margo in on this too.

Angela released her grip. "It's nothing, Mom," she called. "I'll be right there." She turned back toward Carly. "You two go."

"Eddie's hoagie," Carly said, grabbing the bag.

"Leave it," Angela ordered. "I'll get it to him. I could use a break, anyway." She picked up her tray and dashed behind the counter to grab the orders that were piling up.

Carly and Nick slipped down the hall. They cracked open the door and eased out onto the small strip of boardwalk that served as the back alley to all the stores and shops. They climbed over the rail and dropped into the cool sand below.

# CHAPTER 10

"Where are you going?" Nick hissed in the darkness.

"This way," Carly whispered, pointing up the beach. The cool deep sand under the boardwalk was spilling into the sides of her sneakers.

"But don't you live . . . ?"

Carly put her finger to her lips, turned from Nick and began to run. She stayed under the boardwalk, out of sight, the sound of her footsteps muffled by the deep sand. She ran for two blocks, dodging the pilings and the occasional trashcans, never looking back. Breathing hard, she paused under one of the amusement piers and leaned against a wooden piling. It vibrated from the rides and the heavy foot traffic above her head. Laughter and screams, merry-go-round music, and the low hum of conversation drifted down to her.

Standing under the boardwalk on a dark summer night, Carly thought, was like being in a closet in the entryway of a house. People came and went, voices without faces, footsteps without feet, movements all muffled and mysterious. It reminded her of the many childhood hours she had spent confined to closets for spilling her milk, for untied shoelaces, for laziness, stupidity, and "bold looks" she never knew she had. In the beginning she had been terrified, begging to be let out, promising to be good. But as time went on she got used to the darkness and curled up with relief amongst the coats, boots, and other miscellaneous junk. The closet meant that the hitting and shouting were done and she would be left alone. She would sometimes pretend that she was a rabbit, safe in her hole. She lined the floor with her mother's coat and curled up on top of it, rubbing the sleeve down the side of her face until the throbbing went away, losing herself in the smell of peppermints and ivory soap and lavender.

Except for certain times in the summers when she became painfully thirsty and longed for a mouthful of fresh air, she didn't mind the closet all that much. She found things to do in there. She braided the straw on the broom and tied up her hair with the laces from her shoes. She investigated the pockets of all the coats, sometimes finding coins to flip. She made up songs and little poems. Often a cookie or chocolate bar slid silently under the door and she knew that her mother was thinking of her. She was clumsy and slow, stupid and full of mistakes, but in the closet there was no one to see, no one to care.

Carly leaned her head back against the hard wood. A roller coaster rumbled overhead and a tremor ran down the piling and through her back. A figure was moving through the darkness just in front of her. She ducked behind the piling. But it was only Nick, half walking, half running, peering all about. She stepped out into the open.

"What are you doing?" he demanded, huffing. The bright lights from above filtered between the boards and striped the dark sand at his feet.

Carly wrapped her arm around the pole. "I'm trying to lose that guy that's following me."

"Yeah, well, you almost lost me too. I thought you were going to go straight home and tell your parents. Do you live under the boardwalk or something?" Nick's voice was hushed and heavy with fear or anger.

"No." Carly dug the toe of her shoe into the sand. A stripe of light cut across the bridge of Nick's nose, but his eyes were hidden in the darkness. "You don't have to stay with me," she said.

"Oh, right," Nick complained, stepping closer, his voice rising. "I'll just go back and tell Angela that I left you under the amusement pier. Then I won't have to worry about the stalker anymore because my sister will have killed me. Carly, don't you know that this is about the stupidest place you could be? Some guy got knifed down here about five years ago." Nick looked over his shoulder and stuffed his hands in his pockets. "This place gives me the creeps."

"I'm not staying here," Carly argued. "I'm just catching my breath. I only wanted to run under the boardwalk far enough so he wouldn't see me heading for the beach."

"The beach!? What is wrong with you? Are you crazy?

Some strange guy's following you and you're going down to the beach? It's totally dark and deserted out there. You gotta go home and tell your parents. Come on."

Carly didn't move. She was too big now for closets and rabbit holes, and she wasn't afraid of the darkness. She stuck her head out from under the boardwalk. Black clouds swirled past the moon and the sharp wind flung dry sand over the surface of the beach like mist over water. If there had been a full moon draping the shore in a soft glow, she would have had to take Nick's advice. But the clouds were in her favor.

"I'm going, Nick," Carly said. "Just tell Angela that I went home. I'll be fine. It's too dark for anyone to see me out there. Thanks for doing this, you know, for coming out here. It was real nice of you."

"But, Carly ..."

Carly turned and ran toward the ocean. The wind was gusting in great blasts, smacking against her in waves and throwing her off balance. The ocean was loud and frothy. Whitecaps were falling one upon the other, tumbling full of spray onto the shore. Carly took off her shoes and stood at the water's edge, the wind singing in her ears and ballooning her clothes, the ocean foaming around her feet.

"Don't kick me or anything." Carly heard Nick's voice above the din of the waves and turned. He was standing several feet behind her, his hands jammed into his pockets, his baggy blue T-shirt rippling in the wind.

She left the edge of the water and went to him. "What are you doing here?"

"I have no idea," Nick answered, shaking his head. "I must be totally nuts."

They stood silently for a few moments, squinting to keep the blowing sand from their eyes.

"You're sure you don't want me to walk you home?" Nick offered.

"I'm sure," Carly insisted. "I'm staying here."

"Come on, then," Nick said. "Let's climb up into the lifeguard stand and get away from this blowing sand."

Carly climbed up first and scrunched back into the corner of the seat, pulling her knees to her chest.

"I'm coming up now," Nick yelled. "It's just me, Nick D'Angelo. Keep your feet to yourself, okay?" He paused. "You're not mad at me for anything now, are you? I'm safe to climb, right?"

Carly looked down at him in the darkness and smiled. She stuck out her hand and he grabbed it, climbing nimbly up into the seat beside her. She had never been in the stand with anyone before, and she immediately felt the warmth of his body. She was glad for the darkness. She felt her face growing red, and there was a feeling inside her stomach like the kind she got when the car went too fast over a dip in the road. They sat silently for a while, facing the ocean and taking the full blast of the wind in their faces.

Nick began to tremble. "It's getting cold up here. Are you really sure you don't want to go home?"

"I'm not going."

"Why not? Do your parents beat you or something?"

Carly felt a hot flash of fear. Her breath seemed to disappear, and she quickly looked away from Nick.

"Carly?" Nick leaned toward her. "I was just kidding, you know."

But she couldn't look at him for fear the secret was there on her face and he would read it.

"I have an idea." Nick jumped down from the stand. "Come on."

"I'm not leaving. You can go if you want. I don't mind."

"I'm just getting out of the wind. Look." Nick headed for the lifeguard's boat, a big wooden vessel that was overturned next to the stand. Carly jumped down and watched him.

"I used to go under these when I was kid and I ran away from home," Nick explained, tilting the boat a bit on its side. "It was a great place to hide. I think we can both fit."

Carly bent low and peered into the darkness under the boat. "Are you crazy?"

"Hey, it's crazier to sit up on that stand and get blasted by the wind all night."

Carly thought of a little Nick, burrowing in the sand, making a home in the hollow of the boat. She rolled into the cool sand and lay on her back. Nick slipped in beside her and gently lowered the boat over their heads. The darkness was total and it suddenly seemed very quiet with the wind no longer ringing in her ears. It was like being in a tiny cave, safe from the world and the raging weather outside. She lay shoulder to shoulder with Nick, his arm pressed against hers, and listened to his light breathing and the muffled sound of the waves.

"Why'd you run away when you were little?" Carly asked, breaking the silence, her voice sounding strange in the small space under the boat. "Margo seems so great. I can't imagine ever wanting to run away from her."

"My mom's the best. It wasn't that. Things were just sort of different when my dad was around. He and my mom were always yelling at each other and arguing about stuff. I used to sneak out and go down to the beach and hide under one of the lifeguard boats near my house. My mom always knew where to find me. Things got a lot better after my dad left."

Carly was speechless, her heart rising in her throat. She thought of her own home with her father gone. "How did you get him to leave?" she asked finally, her voice no more than a whisper.

Nick turned on his side in the small space, propping his head on his arm. She could just make out his outline in the darkness.

"He just left."

"Oh." A strong blast of wind knocked against the side of the boat and it moved slightly. Carly grabbed a handful of sand and slowly worked it through her fingers.

"He lives in Atlantic City. I can go see him whenever I want. How about you?" Nick asked.

"What?"

"Did you ever run away from home when you were a kid?"

Carly gripped the sand inside her fists. She had, but only once. There was no boat to hide under, no mother to carry her safely home. She had hidden in the wooden castle in the playground, keeping watch through the slats in the tower and munching on crackers she had stolen from the closet. It was dark when he came and she hadn't heard anything until he was right next to her, the anger shooting from him like fire from a dragon. She ended up with a broken arm and a new fairy tale drilled into her head of how she had fallen at the playground in a silly stunt. If she ran away again, it would have to be forever, somewhere she could never be found.

"Well, did you?" Nick persisted.

"It's too hot in here." Carly pushed up at the side of the boat.

"What are you doing?"

"I need some air," Carly gasped.

Nick helped her tilt the boat, and she slithered out from beneath it. The wind blasted against her back, and the goose bumps rose on her arms. Nick was halfway out, shielding his eyes with his left hand and trying to hold the boat up slightly with his right.

"I gotta go," Carly yelled over the wind. The sky was black with swirling clouds. Not a star could be seen. "I'll see you later."

Nick struggled to get his legs from under the boat. "Wait for me!" he called.

Carly heard his words across the wind, but ran on at top speed at the water's edge, his questions trailing her every step. When she got to 33$^{rd}$ Avenue, she headed off the beach toward home, deep in thought. She didn't see the men standing in the shadows of the boardwalk until it was too late.

# CHAPTER 11

"Hello, Carly."

The words stopped her dead in her tracks. Someone stepped out from behind a piling into the dim glow cast by the boardwalk lights. It was the tall man. His hands were in his pockets and he leaned back against the wooden pole. "You're a pretty hard girl to talk to," he said. "Do you know that?"

Carly had been thinking of Nick, and the shock of seeing the tall man momentarily froze her. A chill, like an icy hand, gripped at her insides. She turned to run, but another man she hadn't seen was just behind her. He grabbed her wrist and held it just tightly enough to prevent her from slipping free. She felt a scream rolling inside her like a towering wave, but she didn't know how to get it out. Nick's story about someone getting knifed under the boardwalk flashed through her mind.

"I'm Mr. Jenkins," the tall man explained, "and this is Mr. Fitzgerald. We're Secret Service agents from the Treasury Department. You know what that is?"

Carly took a quick look at their faces and tugged

desperately at her arm to get free.

"It's part of the United States Government. There's nothing for you to worry about. We just want to ask you a few questions, okay?"

Carly looked down at the sand and said nothing. She felt the pressure of the agent's fingers wrapped hard around her wrist. Her hand began to throb in rhythm with her heart.

"We've noticed you making some deliveries around town, Carly, and hanging out on the boardwalk at night. You look like a good kid. I'll bet you help your parents out a lot at home, don't you? Doing chores, helping in the store, right?"

The smaller man, Mr. Fitzgerald, had pulled her under the boardwalk, away from any interested stares from passersby above. Carly gave a few more sharp tugs on her arm.

"Come on, now, Carly. We're not going to hurt you. Just stand still for a few minutes. It's not a big deal here, okay? We're just talking." The tall man reached into his pocket. "Want a piece of gum?" He held a piece out to her, but she turned her head away. "Did your dad give you any money to spend tonight on the boardwalk?"

Carly thought of how empty her pockets were, compliments of Frankie. The idea of her father giving her money to spend on the boardwalk was ridiculous, and she had a strange and almost overwhelming urge to burst out laughing. The tall man stepped closer to her and reached into the front pocket of his jacket. Carly tensed, watching the slow, deliberate movement of his hand. But he only pulled out a small black case. He flipped it open and dangled it in front of her face. Even in the darkness, Carly could see the shine of the badge. Angela's words drifted through her head—any creep can get a badge. How were you supposed to know if a badge was real or not? Either way, she was in big trouble.

"Come on, now, Carly. These aren't hard questions. You help us out a little and we'll help you. Okay?" The tall man stood only inches from her. His clothes were neat and clean and he smelled of pipe tobacco. "What was in that package you delivered on Bay Avenue today? Do you know?"

Carly stood mute. She couldn't have answered even if she wanted to. Her throat was closed tightly, and though the wind was whipping all around her head, she couldn't seem to get any of it into her lungs. Out of the corner of her eye, she saw a shadow moving under the boardwalk.

"It wasn't candy, was it?" the tall man asked, unwrapping the piece of gum he had offered Carly and popping it into his mouth. "Little candy shops don't make deliveries. People who want candy go the store and buy it. Right?"

Carly focused on his shoes, brown loafers with little tassels, sinking in the deep sand. Mr. Fitzgerald loosened his grip a little and the blood started tingling back into her hand.

"Hey, Fitz," the tall man said, "isn't there a curfew for kids in this town?"

"You bet," Fitz answered.

"I've seen you out late a couple of times, Carly," the tall man said. "If you can't answer a few easy questions here, I might have to take you to the police station and try it there."

Just then there was a loud cry and sand came raining down on them. Carly felt herself jerked free from the agent and she stumbled backward into the sand.

"Get up, get up!" Nick yelled. "Run, run!"

Nick had jumped from behind the nearest piling and thrown fistfuls of sand right into the agents' faces. They were rubbing their eyes and coughing. Carly scrambled to her feet and took off behind Nick, sprinting at top speed, off the beach, down back alleys, over damp lawns, turning corners, gulping air until a hot pain ran down her throat and into her chest. They collapsed, panting, behind a small signal house across the railroad tracks. They faced the dark expanse of the marsh, the tall grasses whispering musically in the wind. It was a long time before either one of them dared to speak.

Carly couldn't have felt more strangely if she had fallen through time and ended up in the next century. Nothing was familiar. All she had wanted was to escape her hot bedroom, watch the crowds on the boardwalk, and be near the ocean for a few hours. Everything had gone seriously wrong. Her father was right. Trouble followed her everywhere and even her best intentions were no more than twisted mistakes. She drew her legs up tightly against her body and rested her forehead on her knees.

"Carly?" Nick lightly touched her shoulder.

She slowly lifted her head. The tall reeds were thrashing about in the wind, and the darkness over the marsh was so thick that it looked as though she could grab big armfuls of it and wrap it around herself.

"Are we in serious trouble, or what?" Nick whispered, peering about in the darkness.

"I don't know, I don't know," Carly moaned. She leaned her head back against the wooden boards of the signal house.

"Is it true?"

"What?"

"The stuff those guys were saying to you?"

Carly bit down on her lower lip. "You heard everything?"

"Almost," Nick answered. "It sounds like your dad's in trouble for something."

"How do you know those guys were for real? Remember what Angela said, that anybody can get a fake badge?"

"It didn't sound like they were faking it. I mean, think about it. They didn't try to steal anything or hurt you. They just asked you a bunch of questions."

"They did ask me for money," Carly argued, rubbing her wrist where she had been held. "And, anyway, if you thought that they were so legitimate, why'd you throw sand in their faces?"

"Well, I couldn't be positive, and when the tall guy started talking about taking you in somewhere, I thought it was best to get out of there."

They both sat silently. A light, misty rain began to fall.

"Thanks," Carly said quietly.

"Sure." Nick shrugged and looked down. He picked up a few of the light brown pebbles at his feet and rattled them around in his hand. He gave Carly a sidelong glance. "Throwing things is one of my talents." Nick stood and began to hurl the pebbles, one at a time, out into the marsh. They no sooner left his hand than they were sucked into the darkness, disappearing soundlessly.

"Weren't you afraid?" Carly asked, remembering his leap from behind the piling, fistfuls of sand flying. "What if they had guns?"

"I didn't think about that. They didn't look too scary. They looked like... like... well, like lawyers or stockbrokers or something. Besides, all I kept thinking about was if I just stood there, and they took you away, and you ended up murdered the next day, I'd feel creepy for the rest of my life. Do you have a big sister?"

Carly shook her head.

"Well, I try to stay on Angela's good side. I'd have attacked those guys to save her pet iguana if she told me to."

"Oh." Carly felt an unfamiliar pain spreading across her chest. Nick would have sprung to the rescue for a trapped iguana. It just so happened to be her. "So Angela told you to 'save' me?"

"Well, yeah, sort of. She told me to take care of you and to make sure you got home safe and all because...." Nick picked up another handful of pebbles and resumed flinging them into the darkness.

"Because why?"

"Well, because you're sort of... well... just because."

Carly could think of lots of words to fill in the blank. She had heard them all before—weird, loner, strange, quiet. She had slipped, broken the rules. She had start-ed to think of herself in some small way as Nick's friend. There was an ache growing in her chest that she could hardly bear. She would rather be a stranger than to be his little pet project, like some stray, bedraggled kitten that needed to be bottle-fed, its progress documented in a science report.

"I've gotta go." Carly jumped to her feet.

"Hold on." Nick grabbed her arm and they both stood flat against the signal house, out of the misting rain. "I have an idea."

"What?" Carly looked down at his hand, wrapped around her arm, and he let go.

"We could find out if those two guys are legitimate or not."

"How?"

"We'll look up the Department of Treasury number in the phone book and then we'll call and ask for Mr. Jenkins or Mr. Fitzgerald. If there's nobody there by those names, we'll know they're phony."

"Yeah, but how do you know that the tall guy and his friend didn't just use somebody else's name, some-body who really works at the Treasury Department?"

"Well, if there's nobody there named Mr. Jenkins or Mr. Fitzgerald, we'll know they're imposters for sure. If one of them does get on the line, I think I could recog-nize his voice. C,mon, it's a great idea. It's worth a try. You could meet me tomorrow about one o'clock at my mom's place, and we'll go to a phone booth."

Carly looked away, out into the marsh.

"If it turns out that they're phony, we can get Angela and my mom or your parents to go to the cops with us. If those guys really are officers of some kind, then we might be in some trouble. We'll have to figure out what our story's gonna be. Can you come at one?"

Carly felt trapped, stuck in the corner of a crumbling house. No matter which way she turned, there was no escaping the crash. She wasn't going to go to the police even if the tall man was a serial killer. She would rather take her chances with him than have her father learn that she had been sneaking out. If the tall man was really a government officer, she was in a different kind of trouble. She didn't know what it was, but she knew it was bad.

"I can't come at one," Carly said. "I have to work."

"How about earlier, then?"

Unless she had deliveries to make, Carly knew that there was no way she could get out of the shop. "No. I have to work all day."

"C'mon, what do you mean you have to work all day? Just tell your mom you have to run out to the store or something. You can think of some excuse."

"No," Carly said. "I can't do it." At least rescued iguanas and abandoned kittens weren't expected to talk, to come up with answers that didn't exist. "I gotta go," she said over her shoulder, and took off through the light rain. She ran through shrouded streets, swallowing the cool mist, avoiding the yellow glow that hung from the streetlights like spider's webs heavy with dew.

She crept into the yard and gripped the bottom branch of the tree, swinging her legs up the slippery trunk.

# CHAPTER 12

"Pssssst! Carly!"

Carly dropped to the ground with a soft thud and crouched behind the tree.

"It's only me. Over here."

She peeked across the yard. Aileen was hanging over the white fence that separated their backyards, motioning with her hand. Carly shook her head, but Aileen only called out louder.

Carly sprinted across the grass to the fence. "What do you want?" she demanded in a whisper. "I have to go in."

"You live in the tree?"

Carly didn't have time for this. "I snuck out, okay? That's why I have to get back in. I use the tree instead of the front door. My bedroom's there." Carly turned and pointed up to the third floor window.

"Oh, my God!" Aileen gasped. "You'll kill yourself!"

"I will not. I do it all the time. But he'll kill me if he catches me out here. I have to go."

Aileen reached over the fence and grabbed Carly's arm.

101

"Come over to my house. He won't see you."

"No! Let go." Carly pulled her arm free and headed for the tree.

"If you come, I'll tell you what that tall man said to me today after you ran away," Aileen sang.

Carly stopped in the middle of the yard and turned.

A smile spread across Aileen's face. "Go to the back gate. I'll let you in."

Carly scanned the windows of her house. They were all dark. Five more minutes out probably wouldn't make any difference. She had to know what the tall man said. She crept to the gate and Aileen lifted the latch, letting her into the yard.

"This way." Aileen motioned toward the house.

"No way! Right here." Carly dropped to the ground, her back to the fence. "Tell me here. I can't stay."

A fine mist was still falling, cloaking the trees and shrubs and framing the porch lights with wide halos.

Aileen rested her hands on her hips. "Carly, the ground's all wet. I am not sitting out here. If you want to hear, you have to come inside."

"No! What if your parents see me?" Carly felt the wet seeping through her shorts and she leaned forward onto her knees.

"They won't. They're in the parlor with some of the guests talking about English Literature and dead poets and other such fascinating stuff. Why do you think I was sitting out on the back porch? I can sneak you in with no problem." Aileen took a few steps toward the house. "But, then again, if you don't really care about what that tall guy said, we can just forget it."

Carly sighed. She knew what Aileen was doing, but, like a fly dangling in a spider's web, she was powerless to stop it.

"Okay, Aileen. But, *please*, I can only stay for five minutes."

"Sure. Leave when you want. C'mon." Aileen led the way across the yard, her long skirt trailing in the wet grass. Carly kept to the fence, out of view of her own house, and waited for Aileen to give her the all clear signal before sprinting up the steps and into the back door.

They were in the kitchen. Carly paused while Aileen stole some muffins from the sideboard. It was a beautiful room, polished wood floors, an elegant table, gingerbread curtains on the windows. Three candles burned on the counter and long shadows flickered across the floor. The whole house smelled like cinnamon and dried flowers. Aileen lifted her skirt and tiptoed up a narrow, dark staircase in the back of the kitchen, the muffins cradled in her left arm. Carly followed.

Aileen's room was just at the top of the stairs. They slipped in and Aileen quickly locked the door. "See? Told ya'. Now, isn't this better than being out in the yard?" She put the muffins on a small table that held an old-fashioned pitcher and washbasin and was lined with a hand-stitched doily. She flopped back on her bed. "Have a seat."

There were two twin beds in the room and Carly sat

gingerly on the one across from Aileen. The spreads felt silky and were covered with a bright design of red roses and trailing vines. The heavy curtains matched the spreads and blended with the striped wallpaper.

"I like your room," Carly offered.

Aileen snorted. "It stinks. I'm not even allowed to put up one lousy poster of something that I like. Harry and Sandra would have a heart attack. I try telling them that I prefer living in the 21st century, but *noooo*, we can't have anything out of place in the museum." Aileen kicked off her shoes. "Nobody appreciates my taste around here."

Carly would have traded her dreary attic bedroom for this one in one minute, but she didn't have time for small talk. "So what did that tall man say?"

"Good morning."

"What?"

"Good morning. That's what he said."

"That's it?"

"Well, he watched you run away like an idiot through all those cars, then he crossed the street and walked past me. He said, 'Good morning,' and I said, 'Yeah, you too.' Who was he?"

"You made me come all the way up here just so you could tell me *that?*" Carly sputtered. She sunk her nails into the soft bedspread and felt her face flush. "Thanks a lot. I took a big risk for nothing!" She headed for the door, but Aileen jumped up to block her exit.

"Get out of the way. I have to go," Carly said through clenched teeth.

Aileen leaned against the door and crossed her arms. "Fine, you can be mad. I admit, I was looking for a little company, but I also thought that it was a good chance to show you my room, so..."

Carly made a grab for the doorknob.

Aileen pushed her away. "Let me finish! I wanted to show it to you so that you know it's here and you can come up anytime you need to. There's a key on the back porch under the flowerpot."

Carly glared at her. "I won't need it. Just stop butting into my life." Carly pulled the door halfway open and Aileen slammed it shut.

"Aileen?" There were footsteps in the hall and a soft knock on the door. Carly flattened herself against the wall and held her breath.

"Are you okay, honey?"

Aileen put her finger to her lips and motioned for Carly not to move. "I'm fine, Sandra," she called.

"I thought I heard some shouting. Do you have a friend over?"

Carly violently shook her head. Aileen opened the door a crack and faked a big yawn. "No, that was just me. I'm practicing for the tryouts for the play."

"Is that coming up already?" Sandra's voice was low and soothing, like the hum of bees on a warm day.

"Well, no, but I like to be ready."

"Okay, sweetheart. But don't be too loud, all right? Harry and I are turning in. See you in the morning."

"Goodnight, Sandra." Aileen softly closed the door. She and Carly stood silently, staring at each other, until the footsteps receded and a door down the hall clicked shut.

Carly sank to the floor, adrenaline leaking from her system like blood from a wound. "Listen, Aileen," she began in a tired voice, "I'm sorry for yelling. But you really don't know what you're talking about. Things aren't as bad as you're making them out to be. I don't even know why you care. So can you just drop it?"

Aileen stood silently, her face twisted in a strange expression. She quietly sat on the floor across from Carly and began gathering up the wild mop of her hair with her hands, pulling it as best she could onto the top of her head.

"What are you doing?"

Aileen narrowed her eyes at Carly for a moment and looked her up and down. "Taking a big risk," she sighed. She dropped her chin to her chest and pulled the last bits of hair from the back of her neck. "Take a look."

Carly leaned closer. Several old scars crisscrossed over the pale skin of Aileen's neck, raised lumps of pink like tiny mountain ranges, a map of unerasable injuries. Carly stared, unmoving, her mouth dry.

Aileen let her hair fall back into place and shook her head. "I never even showed that to Alexa, not to anybody around here."

Carly heard a toilet flush somewhere down the hall and the low voices of two people coming up the stairs. There was a fumble of keys and soft laughter. A door creaked open and closed. Aileen sat perfectly still, like a wax figure, her eyes fixed on the wall just above Carly's head.

"It's from when I lived in New York," she whispered. "She said she had to do it, to straighten me out, to make me stop being so bad." Aileen held out her right hand. A thin white scar wove its way across her knuckles. "This was to stop me from stealing." A sad smile played across her face. "Didn't quite work, though, did it?"

A lump rose in Carly's throat. She thought of the small, stooped woman she saw so often filling the birdfeeders, weeding the flower garden, and warmly greeting the guests at her bed-and-breakfast inn. Maybe Aileen was only acting again, sucking Carly in with a string of lies. "Sandra did that?" she asked, not hiding the edge in her voice.

Aileen jerked her head up. "No, of course not. It was Dolores, one of my foster mothers." Aileen ran her hands through her hair and brushed invisible lint from her skirt, as though trying to shake off the memory that had unexpectedly spilled from her. Her knees were nervously jerking back and forth beneath her long skirt and her hair was standing on end. She cracked each of her fingers before continuing. "Harry and Sandra came later. They were my last foster parents, because then they adopted me."

"You're adopted?"

Aileen flexed her right hand and the scar rose and fell over her knuckles. "Yeah, but I was at a lot of places before that." She fingered the scar, as though trying to smooth it out of her skin, then looked up at Carly.

"Just don't ever try to tell me that I don't know what I'm talking about, okay? I know ten times more stuff than the people around here."

Carly looked away from the scar that ran like a boundary line through the middle of Aileen's hand. Do not cross. Danger. "It's not that bad in my house," she insisted. "It's just not." After all, her broken arm had healed, her bruises always faded away. She lived with her parents in Oceanside, not in some broken-down foster home in New York. She had a family. It wasn't perfect, but whose was? There wasn't anywhere else for her to go, anyway. Aileen's situation was different. Totally different.

Aileen drew her knees up under her chin. "It'll get worse," she said. "Unless you do something about it, it will definitely get worse."

Carly rested her head back against the wall. She closed her eyes and fought back the nausea that was rising in her stomach. Were things getting steadily worse? She never thought of it that way, never measured the year to year decline in their relationship. It felt more to her like a roller coaster than a big slide, with unexpected sharp turns and sudden drops. She was taking huge risks this summer by sneaking out of the house and shuddered to think of the steep fall if he ever found out. But Aileen was wrong. There was nothing to "do" about it but to hold on and ride it out.

"So what are you going to do?" Aileen asked.

Carly opened her eyes. "There's nothing I can do, okay? Even if I wanted to do something, which I don't."

"Well, there's something I can do," Aileen said. "I can tell, if you won't."

Carly stood up. "Don't! If you do, I swear I'll tell about that makeup you stole on the boardwalk." Carly felt a twinge of guilt as Aileen's face fell, but she had no choice. She had to protect herself. "Listen, Aileen," she added hurriedly, "I know you're just trying to help me, but it wouldn't help. It would make things worse. Besides, nobody would believe you anyway."

Aileen sniffed. "Sandra and Harry would believe me."

"Don't," Carly warned. "Just don't. I can handle my own problems. I gotta go."

"Fine." Aileen grabbed one of the muffins that she had pilfered from the kitchen and began to carefully peel the paper cup from its bottom. "But I'll be watching."

Carly slipped out into the hall, tiptoed down the steps and out through the dim kitchen.

A misty rain was still falling, but she had no problem scaling the tree. She paused on the roof to glance at the house next door. Aileen was watching her, framed in the window, her hair spread out from her head like the mane of a lion.

# CHAPTER 13

The morning was cloudy, the streets wet. Carly wiped down the inside front window.

"Watch those displays," her father called from behind the counter. "Don't knock anything over."

"Where's Mom?" Carly asked. Her mother, usually busy in the shop this time of day, had been missing all morning.

"She's not feeling well, that's all. You just worry about getting your work done."

Carly sighed and turned back to the window, staring out at the gray day. The sidewalks were mostly empty. An occasional brave beachgoer, in sandals and a sweatshirt, wandered toward the ocean. The arcades would be full on a day like this and lines for the movies would snake halfway down the block.

"Carly!" her father yelled.

Carly jumped, knocking over a tin of jellies.

"Pick it up." He pushed back the stool from the counter where he sat with a calculator and some papers. "Is it going to take you ten years just to wash one window? Get over here." He came from behind the counter and grabbed the back of her shirt. He yanked her backward. Carly stumbled, the collar of her blouse biting into her neck.

"Look at that," he said, pointing at the glass. "Look at all those streaks. Do you ever pay attention to one single thing that you're supposed to be doing? Do you?" He gave her a small shove toward the window. "I just told you that your mother's feeling sick. You think you would at least have a little consideration for her and try to help out. Fix that window. And when you're done, those boxes in the storage room need to be unpacked." He returned to his stool and hunched over the calculator. He cursed the numbers under his breath and pulled on his chin with his left hand.

The door swung open and a family with three small children entered the shop.

"Good morning!" Mr. Chambers greeted them, dropping his pencil and manufacturing a broad, warm smile. "How are you today?"

"Just fine." The woman removed a crumpled rain hat and shook it out.

Carly saw her father's eyes narrow as they followed the water drops down to the clean floor, but his smile never changed.

"How can I help you?" Mr. Chambers clicked off the calculator and turned on his "aren't they cute?" face as he looked at the three children. He had it down pat, from the crinkle around his eyes to the slight cock of his head. She imagined him practicing each of his many faces in the bathroom mirror, switching into and out of them as quickly as costumes.

"We'd like a pound of fudge, half chocolate nut and half vanilla."

"Coming right up." Mr. Chambers chatted with the woman about the weather, beach erosion, and the rising cost of rentals while he made up the box. The woman's husband spent those five minutes frantically following the children around the store, trying to prevent them from grabbing all the merchandise from the shelves.

"Oh, no," the father moaned. "Add one of those whale lollipops to the bill."

The woman turned from the register. "Why?"

"Because Jenna got one in her mouth when I wasn't looking." The man scooped the little girl up into his arms and the two other children began begging for a lollipop as well. "Better make that three lollipops," he said to Mr. Chambers.

"Those'll be on the house," Mr. Chambers laughed. "My treat. Don't worry about it."

"Hey, thanks a lot. That's real nice of you," the man said.

The bell tinkled as the family left the store and headed up the street. Carly shook her head at their retreating figures. It always amazed her how charming he could be when he wanted, all sweet and smooth like a vanilla butter cream. He sweet-talked customers for the extra business it would bring and waitresses for the special service he got. He played the caring father for Carly's teachers whenever they expressed concern about her silence or her bruises. Carly often wished that she had inherited this talent from him, but she didn't. Would things be different if she could charm her father like he charmed his customers?

Carly set to work on the window. She had just squirted the cleaner onto the glass when she saw him between the blue liquid streaks. She grabbed a paper towel and wiped furiously. Nick was coming. She hopped back from the window, out of his sight. She prayed he wouldn't come in, that he was headed somewhere else.

The door swung open, the tinkle filled the shop, and Nick was there, his baseball cap crooked and a huge grin spreading across his face. "Hey, Carly!" he called, his cheerful voice bouncing off the walls.

Carly felt her eyes growing huge and her heart was crashing against her chest. She wondered if her father could hear it. His stool scraped back from the counter. Panic flooded her body and she worried desperately that, like a leaky dam, it was seeping out of her some-where and her father would see. She caught Nick's eye and frantically mouthed the word *No*.

"Who are you?" Mr. Chambers asked, stepping for-ward, not bothering with his usual customer face.

"He's Nick D'Angelo. He's just a kid who..."

"Was I talking to you?" Mr. Chambers boomed at Carly. "You keep your mouth shut unless I'm talking to you."

Nick gave Carly a quick, startled look. She stood, her mouth half open, clutching the Windex bottle and the damp paper towel. Her body felt as though it were on fire. She wished that it was and she could disappear, a puff of black smoke, through the crack under the door.

Mr. Chambers turned back toward Nick. "Now, who are you?"

"I'm Nick D'Angelo."

"I heard that. I'm not deaf. How do you know my daughter's name and what are you doing here?"

Carly winced. Her father had driven away a number of children who had come to ask her to play when she was little. Pesky, annoying little brats who wasted their time and didn't mind wasting other people's as well, he always said. She had been sad to see them go, but with Nick it was a different feeling. It was a strange ache, like a precious egg she had hidden inside was being smashed, and all that was worth saving was oozing away.

"Look, I just came to get some candy for my mom for her birthday," Nick stuttered, reaching for the door handle. "But if it's such a big deal, forget it. I'll get it somewhere else."

Nick had the door open a few inches. Mr. Chambers reached his long arm over Nick's head and thrust it shut. "Answer my question. How do you know my daughter's name?"

Nick was backed into the corner and Carly couldn't see his face. She dropped the Windex bottle to the floor and kicked it forward, pretending clumsiness. Her father turned for a second and Carly caught Nick's eye. Lie, lie, she tried to say to him with her look. She couldn't tell if he understood. His face was full of confusion.

"Uh..., let's see," Nick began. "We were in math class

together this year, and last year we had the same social studies and English teachers."

Mr. Chambers backed away. "Get your candy and get out," he barked. He turned toward Carly. "Is this one of those kids that throws sand at you?"

Carly shook her head. Only at Secret Service agents, she thought. Carly moved behind the counter and stared down at the candy. She was afraid to meet Nick's eyes again for fear her father would see that Nick was more than just some kid from her math class.

"My mom likes licorice," Nick said, peering into the display case. "But I've only got five bucks to spend."

"I'll make up a box," Carly said quietly. Her father had moved just behind her. She stole a quick glance at Nick. His mouth was a tight, thin line, his hands shoved deep into his pockets. She fumbled with the licorice mixture and spilled some into a small white box. Nick slid a five-dollar bill across the counter. She felt her hands shaking as she counted out the change from the register. Her father stood over her, watching, and suddenly the numbers all left her mind. She fingered the quarters and then the dimes, forgetting what Nick had given her.

"For God's sake!" her father cried, reaching his hand into the drawer. "Sixty-three cents. I don't know how the hell you got past the second grade. Here." He thrust the money at Nick.

Carly saw that her mother had drifted down the stairs into the shop and stood, like a shadow, against the wall. Carly looked toward her, but her mother only bit her lower lip and dropped her eyes to the floor.

Nick backed toward the door. "Okay, well, see ya around, like—I mean, next year in school or something."

Mr. Chambers came from around the counter and slowly opened the door. "You stay away from Carly," he said in a low, threatening voice. Nick barely got out of the way before the door slammed behind him.

Carly passed her silent mother, headed straight for the storage room and dropped onto the floor, her head in her hands. She was trembling and she wasn't sure if it was because she came so close to getting caught or because she felt totally humiliated. She could never look at Nick again. Never. She pulled the UPS box toward her and ripped the packaging tape off. She tore open the cardboard. It was probably for the best anyway. She knew from the start that someone like Nick wouldn't waste much time on someone like her. She slammed her hand into the box and scattered the Styrofoam peanuts. Better it ended now. It would hurt far worse if she pretended through the rest of the summer that he was her friend. She pulled the containers from the box, candies that they didn't make but ordered from a supplier and sold at a higher price to make a profit. She stacked them on the metal shelves that were jammed against the back wall.

The phone was ringing in the office. She heard her father's voice, low at first, then rising in anger. A flash of panic ran through her. What if Margo knew what happened and was calling to complain about how Nick had been treated? She tiptoed out of the storage room and inched her way down the corridor. The office door was open halfway.

"How could you be so stupid?!" he yelled. "I want to know every single thing that happened. And don't leave anything out."

Carly stood frozen against the wall in the silence for several minutes. It wasn't Margo, or her father wouldn't be listening so quietly for so long. But she didn't leave. She thought of the questions the tall man had asked her. She had never really wondered much about what her father did. Everywhere they lived he was into something different and she stopped trying to keep track of his projects. Carly's mother explained that he was restless and had to follow after every "new opportunity."

When they first moved to Oceanside, Carly didn't find it strange at all that she was not permitted in the cellar. Her father had always had a private space where he worked and she was not allowed. She didn't care what he was doing each night, as long as it left her free. But now the tall man planted a seed in her head. She tried to ignore it, but it was growing anyway.

"Wait. Stop," she heard her father break in. "I'll tell you exactly what you're going to do. Tomorrow I'll send—hold on—" His voice dropped. "Close that door, Leila."

The office door quietly closed and Carly slipped back into the storage room. She sat on the floor and leaned her head on one of the boxes. She closed her eyes for a few minutes and dreamed of the ocean, straining to hear the rhythm of the waves.

But something felt wrong. Carly sat up quickly and opened her eyes. Her father stood in the doorway, watching her. He had a red splotch under his right eye and one on his left cheek. She jumped to her feet and began to open the next box.

"Leave it," he said quietly. "It doesn't matter anymore. We're moving."

"What?!" Carly turned quickly, her hands still on the box.

"You heard me. We're moving." He folded his arms across his chest. "Soon."

"We can't! I don't want to move!" Carly blurted, more to herself than to him. Before she even had time to flinch, he unfurled his right arm from his chest and struck her sharply across the face with the back of his hand. The edge of his ring caught under her cheekbone and opened up a gash. Carly made no sound, but dropped to the floor and held her face. She felt the warm blood ooze between her fingers and slowly roll down her arm. The sharp sting on her face brought tears to her eyes, but they were too shallow to spill out and quickly dried to nothing.

Carly felt a hand on her shoulder and jumped, but it was only her mother. "Come on, honey," she said softly. "Let's go upstairs and fix that up."

"I don't want to move," Carly whispered into her hands. "Why can't we stay here?"

"It's just time to go," her mother said.

"When?" Carly asked.

Mrs. Chambers went to the door and checked the hallway, then came back to help Carly to her feet. "As soon as we can," she said. "As soon as we can."

# CHAPTER 14

Carly lay on her bed in the evening, the small lamp that sat beside her bed, propped on an overturned milk crate, on low. The fan hummed in the corner. She ran her fingers down the side of her face, exploring. The bruise was sore and starting to swell, but she'd had worse. Just another little "accident," as her mother would say.

Dinner was more uncomfortable than usual. Her father acted as though nothing had happened and tried to make small talk. Carly refused to say a word, to even notice that he existed. She played around with her food, endlessly shaping and crushing her mashed potatoes. But she felt slightly guilty about her silence too, because whenever she looked up from her plate, she saw the strain on her mother's face, the small forced smiles, the deep lines around her eyes.

Mrs. Chambers was worn thin trying to hold a husband and a daughter together, while every year the chasm between them grew. It was a hopeless task. Sometimes Carly wondered if it wasn't all her own fault, if things would be different if only she tried harder. Her mother always begged her to forgive him for the "accidents," to understand that he didn't mean them and that he loved her. But she didn't understand and the forgiveness wasn't in her.

Carly jumped up and sat on the edge of her bed, sweating. Her room was sweltering hot. She had thought about staying in tonight, avoiding Nick and the tall man, and hiding her bruised face. But she couldn't do it. If she were moving soon, she might have only a few nights left.

Worried that Nick's appearance at the store today could have raised her father's suspicions, she took two blankets from the top of her closet and all the clothes from her drawer. She arranged them in a pile under her covers in the shape of her own body. She unplugged the light. She fingered the small latch lock on her door, but left it undone. It wouldn't hold against his strong push anyway. If he came to check on her, she hoped he would crack open the door and be satisfied with the dark, unmoving figure on the bed. As a last precaution, she tore off a long piece of Scotch tape and pressed it across the edge of the door and onto the wall. If he came to her room for any reason, the tape would be torn from the wall and she would at least know that he had been there.

Carly made a final adjustment to her dummy, then slipped through the window and crawled to the edge of the roof. The tree was thick, but she knew before she climbed very far that something wasn't right. There was a flash of color below her and she froze. She heard a rustling, then the snap of a branch and a murmured curse. Carly leaned toward the trunk and peeked through an opening in the leaves. There was a tangled mass of red hair far below, nestled among the branches like an untidy bird's nest.

"Aileen!" Carly hissed. "What are you doing?"

"I'm coming for a visit," Aileen sang, her voice dangerously loud. "How *do* you do this? I can't get past the first branch."

Carly made her way down nimbly, quickly moving from limb to limb, her heart pounding. "Get out!" she whispered. "Are you crazy?"

"I think I'm stuck." Aileen scratched at her head. "Are there any bugs in my hair?"

Carly tried to peer through the branches at her house. She was sitting about eye level with the storage room window and it wasn't even dusk yet. A cold sweat was breaking out all over her body. "Aileen, I'm not kidding. We have to get out of here right now!"

Aileen swung her legs through the empty air and stared at the ground. "I can't," she murmured. "I don't know how." She looked up at Carly, her eyes wide. "I'll tell you what, though. This whole experience has given me a new respect for squirrels."

Carly was breathing quickly. "If you make a sound, I'll kill you. We have to do this fast. Kick off your clogs."

Aileen's shoes dropped softly into the grass.

"Now turn around like this, and hook your arms over the branch." Carly dangled from the tree, in plain view.

"I can't, I can't," Aileen whined.

"Do it! I swear I'll push you off if you don't!"

Aileen hung beside Carly, a low moan in her throat. Carly jumped to the ground. "Drop!" she commanded. "Right now!"

Aileen tumbled out of the tree with a small cry and Carly grabbed her arm and dragged her out of the yard. They collapsed on the curb halfway up 34th Street, their backs against a telephone pole.

"You almost killed me," Aileen panted.

"What?!" Carly shouted. "You're the one who almost got me killed! That may have been the stupidest thing you ever did in your life!"

Aileen sat quietly for a moment, staring at her feet. Her toenails were painted with a sparkly purple polish that matched her eye shadow. "I was just coming for a little visit," she grumbled. "I've seen you climb that tree, and it didn't look so hard. I thought I could do it."

Carly sighed. "I never tried climbing a tree in clogs and an ankle length skirt."

"Yeah, well, I didn't know I needed a special wardrobe." Aileen brushed off the bottom of her feet and slipped into her clogs. "Anyway, maybe next time I'll just come in the front door."

Carly jumped to her feet. "You know you can't do that. Just leave me alone, okay? You're going to get me in a lot of trouble."

"Looks like you're already in a lot of trouble. What happened to your face?"

Carly's hand shot up to her bruise and she turned away. "I fell."

"Oh, yeah? Where?"

"In my house."

"I don't believe you."

"I don't care if you do or not. It's none of your business," Carly snapped. She tried to walk away, but Aileen grabbed her shoulder.

"I'm usually not a snitch," she said, "but I'm not keeping quiet anymore. That thing is really big. I'm telling Sandra about this—tonight."

Carly whirled around. Aileen's eyes were narrow, her arms crossed tightly on her chest. The thin white scars on her hands stood out plainly. "Don't do it, Aileen," Carly begged. "You don't need to. I have a plan, and I'm working things out on my own."

Aileen snorted. "I'm telling you, Carly, it never works out on its own."

"Just give me two weeks, okay? Then you can tell anybody you want. You can publish it in the newspaper for all I care."

"Why two weeks?"

"I have my reasons." Carly knew she'd be long gone in two weeks and nothing Aileen did or said would make any difference then.

Aileen pulled a piece of gum from a small bag that was tied around her waist. She popped the gum into her mouth, chewing like a cow, staring at Carly. "All right," she finally said. "You've got fourteen days. Then I'm telling Sandra."

"Okay. I gotta go." Carly took off for the boardwalk before Aileen could change her mind.

She ran for only half a block. The night was too humid and close. The air seemed to be hung with water, and the people moved through it slowly, their faces flushed and glistening in the oppressive heat. Carly hopped up on the stool next to Eddie's stand.

"Hey, Eddie," Carly called, careful only to show him the unbruised left side of her face. "How's it going?"

"Man, it's brutal in here," Eddie sighed. "I wish the darned hurricane would just hit us and put us out of our misery."

"Hurricane!?" Carly stole a quick glance at Eddie. Beads of sweat rolled down his face. He had a white towel wrapped around his neck, but his navy shirt was damp and clung to his body.

"Don't you ever watch the news, girl? Here." Eddie handed her a copy of the local paper. Carly read the headline: EARLY SEASON HURRICANE ANNIE HEADS UP COAST.

"When's it coming?" Carly asked.

"Who knows?" Eddie mopped his face with the end of the towel. "It's supposed to be stalled just south of Virginia. It might even turn out to sea and miss us altogether. I'd almost welcome it if it would clear this darn humidity out of here."

A lady with her hair up in a bun, frizzled pieces sticking out all over like a cactus with a perm, stopped to pick up a paper. She slid fifty cents to Eddie.

"Tell you what, though," Eddie said as the woman moved on, "the threat of a hurricane sure sells a lot of newspapers. I'll probably run out tonight." He nodded toward the departing customer. "Teacher," he said. "I can always pick them out."

"No way!" Carly argued. "I'm the one who goes to school and sees what teachers look like. That was not a teacher. Computer programmer."

"Couldn't be." Eddie shook his head. "She had perfectly polished long nails. How could you sit at a computer all day and not chip those?"

"I don't know." Carly shrugged. "They're probably not real. You should see some of the girls in my computer class. They type pretty fast with just the tips of their nails. Their fingers never even touch the keys." Carly held out her hands and looked down at her bitten nails. She remembered with a sudden chill that this was a bad habit she shared with her father. She closed her hands into fists and dropped them onto her lap.

The next customer bought a racing magazine. His three kids were standing behind him, furiously licking ice cream cones that were melting faster than they could eat them.

"Salesman," Eddie said, after the man moved on.

"Professional photographer," Carly countered.

"Sorry, but I got you on that one," Eddie insisted.

"How do you know?" Carly complained. "Did he give you his card or something?"

"Sort of. He sells auto parts in the Pep Boys store on Route 49. I shop there sometimes."

"Hey, that's cheating! You're disqualified on that last one."

"Okay, okay." Eddie leaned back in the booth and laughed. "I'll forfeit all my prize money to you."

Carly knew just what she would do with it too. She'd head right over to Rita's Water Ice and buy a large, cool gelati. Lots of people had the same idea. There were at least ten customers waiting in line. Carly watched the families come and go, mothers with sons, fathers and daughters, toddlers getting the cool dessert spooned into their mouths by doting parents.

"Do you ever see your son on the boardwalk?" Carly asked, scanning the faces of the passing teenage boys for any who might resemble Eddie.

"Sometimes."

"Would you point him out to me if you saw him?"

"No." Eddie's answer was short and curt. He dumped the change from his apron into the bucket and handed the bucket to Carly.

She knew he was trying to end the conversation, but she just couldn't bear to think of Eddie's son wandering around out there not knowing about his father. It wasn't right. "Do you see him other places, too?"

Eddie silently fingered the edges of the newspapers. "I go to some of his ball games," he finally said, more to himself than in answer to her question. "His mom sends me school photos and copies of his report cards once in a while."

"You've got to tell him who you are!" Carly pleaded. "How can you stand seeing him and not letting him know that you're his dad?"

Eddie shook his head. "It's too late," he said quietly.

"Maybe I should've done something when he was little—been his dad then. But it's too late now. I got my life. He's got his life. I would just mess everything up." He looked up at Carly. "How would you feel if some big, fat newspaperman showed up on your front step and said he was your father? Think about it. I can't do that to the kid."

Several customers lined up at the stand and Carly sat quietly, rocking back and forth on the stool. She felt a little guilty knowing she would be tempted to trade in her own father, abandon him just as Eddie had done to his son. How would she feel in this small town, passing him on the street and treating him like a stranger?

"Good evening, Eddie," said the next customer in a cheery voice.

Carly froze. The tall man stood just in front of her.

"How you doing tonight?" Eddie responded, shooting a quick glance at Carly.

"Pretty good, pretty good. Haven't run into any sudden sand squalls tonight, so I guess I'm doing okay." He looked over at Carly and winked and she felt her heart drop into the bottom of her stomach. "I'll take a copy of the *Inquirer*," he said, sliding his change across the small ledge. "Got to get the latest on old Annie. Think she's going to get us?"

"Maybe," Eddie replied. "Maybe not."

"Well, you two have a good night." The tall man folded his paper and casually walked off down the boardwalk.

Eddie looked at Carly. "Secret Service agent," he said, quietly.

127

Carly's eyes grew wide, but her throat was closed tight and she couldn't disagree.

"He was here last night too," Eddie said. "Seemed like a pretty nice guy. He wanted to look through my bills, mostly at the tens and twenties. I said it was okay with me, as long as he didn't take any. I guess I came out clean. You have any idea what's going on?"

"No." Carly looked up the boardwalk, but the tall man had already disappeared into the throng. Good riddance. She wouldn't let him ruin one of the last nights she might ever have on the boardwalk.

Carly gripped the underside of the stool while two new customers browsed the magazine rack, bought nothing, then moved on.

"Give me your best guess on those last two," Eddie said, changing the subject.

"I wish they were police officers," Carly moaned, stiffening. She saw Frankie Marzano and two of his friends headed right for the stand.

# CHAPTER 15

"Hey, it's our good friend, Carly," Frankie sang out, approaching the stand.

She didn't try to run because that would have meant leaving Eddie all alone. Frankie's friends, Justin and Mark, picked up some magazines and started flipping through the pages, but Frankie came to stand just in front of Carly.

"Look, boys," Eddie growled, "if you want to buy something, buy it. Otherwise, move on."

"Oh, sure," Frankie answered. "We're going to buy something. We're just a little short on cash right now. But Carly will lend us some. She likes to do that."

Frankie made a grab for the bucket of change on Carly's lap. She twisted away and wrapped her arms tightly around it. But Frankie was on it in a minute, trying to wrestle it out of her grasp. He gave a strong yank and the stool toppled over. Carly fell hard to the boardwalk and the coins flew in every direction.

"Hey! Hey! What are you doing?" Eddie was shouting.

All three boys were stuffing change into their pockets and howling with laughter.

"Give that money back. That doesn't belong to you! Carly, are you okay!?" Eddie was trying to maneuver himself off the stool in his booth.

Frankie paused for a moment and looked down at the fistful of change in his hand. "You want your money, fat man? Okay, here it is."

Frankie flung the money at Eddie, coins pelting him in the face and pinging against the side of the stand. Carly jumped to her feet.

Two men came running toward the stand. "What's going on here?" they shouted. "What are you kids doing?"

Frankie and his friends took off, but not before stealing Carly's stool. "Big fat whale!" Frankie called. He held the stool over his head like a trophy, ran a little way up the boardwalk, then dumped it over the side into the sand below.

"You okay?" one of the men asked Carly. She nodded. The other man was trying to convince Eddie to call the police and report the boys. Eddie thanked them for helping but refused to call the police, and the men rejoined their families.

Carly stood in front of the stand window. Eddie sat limply, his head bowed, breathing heavily.

"I'm sorry," Carly said quietly. "If it wasn't for me sitting here, none of this would have happened." She looked around at the mess. One of the magazine racks had been knocked over, coins were scattered everywhere and all the color had drained from Eddie's face. He held his hand to his chest.

"Don't you be sorry. It's my fault," Eddie said bitterly.

"It's all my fault." A tear ran down his face, and he quickly used the end of the towel to wipe it away. Eddie looked up at Carly and his puffy eyes grew wide. "You're bleeding!" he cried.

Carly put her hand to her face and felt the sticky blood oozing from the gash on her cheek. The fall to the boardwalk must have opened it up.

"Maybe I *should* call the police on him if he's capable of that kind of thing," Eddie lamented.

"No, no, Frankie didn't do it," Carly explained. "I got that cut earlier today. I... I... walked into the side of a door. I was just... I wasn't looking where I was going."

"Let me see." Eddie took her chin gently in his hand and turned her face. "That's looking kind of ugly. You better go clean it up."

"In a minute," Carly said, pulling back, her face flushed. She got down on her hands and knees and began to pick up the scattered coins, dropping them in the bucket.

"Forget that!" Eddie yelled.

"It'll just take a minute." Carly knew Eddie wouldn't be able stoop down to pick up all this change, and it amounted to quite a few dollars. She couldn't just leave it there. As she reached for two quarters resting against the stand, another hand darted in front of hers and grabbed them. Carly jumped backward and almost spilled the bucket again.

"Hi," Nick said, plucking up more coins and tossing them into the bucket. "What happened here?"

"Frankie Marzano happened here," Carly sputtered, quickly turning her face away from Nick.

"Frankie Marzano? That little twit? What did he do this for?"

"I'm not the most popular kid in school, in case you never noticed," Carly snapped. A drop of blood fell from her cheek and hit her leg. She quickly wiped it away with the back of her hand. "It's not like he needs a reason to be a jerk, anyway," she sighed.

"Oh my God!" Nick suddenly shouted. "Look at your face! Did Frankie do that?"

"No. I...um...I walked into a door."

Eddie was fanning himself with a magazine. "Will you make her stop picking up those coins?" he begged Nick.

"Yeah," Nick answered. "Carly, sit down, will ya? I got this. No problem."

Leaning over was making her face throb and the blood drip faster. Carly sat back against the stand, out of the way of the customers, as Nick scrambled all about with the bucket picking up the change.

"He was probably drunk," Nick remarked, reaching to get a coin wedged between the boards.

"Drunk!?" Eddie leaned his head out of the window of his stand. "He's only thirteen!"

Nick looked at Carly and shrugged. "Everybody knows Frankie drinks."

"I didn't," Carly said.

"Yeah. He was our first baseman. He was pretty good too. But the coach finally threw him off the team because he was coming to practice loaded and cursing everybody out. Once he got into a fight with Greg Steinart and swung a bat at his head. If Steinart hadn't gotten out of the way, he'd have been dead. Frankie was gone after that."

Eddie's mouth hung open like he'd just seen the whole incident unfold before his eyes. "What about his parents?" he asked. "Don't they do anything?"

"His dad's a real jerk," Nick said. "He coached our team in fourth and fifth grade. He treated Frankie like some major league star. He could do no wrong. He never benched him. He'd let him play any position he wanted. It was really annoying. One time, Frankie cursed out the umpire for calling him out on strikes. You know what his dad did? He gave him a wink and big thumbs up."

"Where's he get the beer?" Eddie sputtered, ignoring a customer who stood, bill in hand, waiting to pay for a magazine.

"I guess he steals it from home," Nick said. "That's what we figure. He sure couldn't pass for twenty-one, even with a fake ID."

Eddie made change for the customer without a word. He leaned out of the stand and looked down at Carly. "Will you get her out of here?" he said to Nick. "She needs to get that cut fixed up and she won't listen to me."

"It's okay, really," Carly insisted.

"No, it's not. You're bleeding all over the boardwalk. You'll scare my customers away."

"Come on, Carly," Nick said, throwing the last of the retrieved coins in the bucket and handing it to Eddie.

Carly jumped up quickly. "I'm just going to go home," she said. "I'll fix it up there."

"No, you're not." Nick grabbed her hand. "Did you know my mom used to be a nurse? She keeps all kinds of bandages and stuff in the closet at the shop. Come on."

Carly stood still and Nick tugged on her arm. "I'm just going to go home," she said.

"No, you're not," he repeated. "I want to buy you a soda too. Maybe we could go down to the beach. It's not as windy as last time."

Without a word and against her better judgment, Carly let him lead her up the boardwalk, the promise of the beach eroding all her resolve.

# CHAPTER 16

"Oh, sweetie! What happened here?" Margo ducked under the counter and, just as Eddie had done, took Carly's chin in her hand and slowly inspected her face. Then she quickly turned. "Nick, I got two pizzas in number one. Table three's waitin' on drinks. Angela, watch the register."

Margo took Carly by the elbow and led her to the back booth. "Sit here." Carly knew it was useless to argue.

Margo went into the storage closet and came out with a very official looking first-aid kit. She snapped it open and slid into the seat beside Carly. She pulled out a damp cloth treated with antiseptic and began to clean around the wound.

"Well," Margo said, her face inches from Carly's, "it's not too deep. I think you'll get away without stitches. How'd you do this?"

"I... I walked into a door," Carly said quickly. "It was real stupid. I just wasn't watching where I was going."

"A door?" Margo leaned back a bit and looked Carly in the eyes.

Carly avoided the gaze and dropped her eyes to her lap. "It was the edge part of the door," she said quietly.

Margo sat silently staring at her for a few moments and then resumed cleaning the wound. Carly felt the blood rushing to her face and she closed her eyes, hoping Margo wouldn't see her humiliation.

"I don't need any bandage, please," Carly protested as Margo attempted to place one on her face.

"Honey, you have to keep this wound clean. You don't want any sand or dirt getting in there and giving you an infection. Okay?"

Carly nodded. She could always pull it off before she got home.

Margo put the bandage on Carly's face, then pulled a pad and pencil from the front pocket of her apron. She quickly wrote something, then tore off the sheet and pressed it into Carly's hand. "If you're ever in any trouble or just need a place to go, you come right here or to my house. I put the address and the phone number on that paper. If you can't come, you call and I'll come get you."

Margo took Carly's shoulders in her hands. Damp strands of hair clung to the sides of her face and flour smudged her lined forehead. But her steely gray eyes were sharp and they locked on Carly's. "Promise me," she urged.

"Okay," Carly muttered. "I will." But she didn't promise. She couldn't do that. She pulled her eyes from Margo's and slipped the paper in her pocket.

"Now you sit there and rest for a few minutes."

And Margo was off again, behind the counter, ringing up a customer, gently chiding Nick for an overdone pizza, sliding orders across the counter to Angela. Carly watched for a few minutes, warm and comfortable in the booth. Nick was filling sodas. Angela, tray high above her head, winked at her mother over some private joke. Margo, even in the midst of thanking customers and checking ovens, was never too busy to rest a hand on Nick's shoulder from time to time.

With a sudden pain in her chest Carly thought of how all this would soon be gone, nothing but a memory. She didn't even know where her family was moving—probably to some dreary city or suburb where there'd be oceans of blacktop and waves of cars, with strip malls instead of boardwalks and no one to care if she wore a bandage on her face. She jumped up from the booth, the urge to run tingling through her legs, and headed toward the boardwalk.

"Hey, Carly, wait!" Nick called before she could leave the shop. He turned and looked at his mother.

"Go on," Margo said to him. "I don't really need you tonight."

Carly looked at the packed booths and the line waiting for take-out and she knew Margo was lying. Margo punched open the register and slipped some bills in Nick's back pocket while he was filling up two cups with soda.

"Thanks, Mom," Nick said, pecking her on the cheek and ducking under the counter.

"Here." Nick handed Carly a large cup. "It's Coke. I hope that's what you wanted."

"Yeah." Carly took a sip from the straw. "It's fine."

As they headed across the boardwalk, Carly saw Aileen in the distance, sitting alone on a bench.

"Come on," Carly urged Nick, and hurried down the steps into the sand, toward the darkness.

But Aileen had seen them. "Hey, Carly!" she shouted. "Thirteen days and twenty-three hours! I'm counting!"

Nick paused. "What's that supposed to mean?"

"Nothing," Carly answered, her head down. "Just keep walking."

Nick shoved his hand in his pocket and did a fake shiver. "That girl is so freaky."

Carly felt her teeth clench, and she gave Nick a sharp shove in the shoulder, nearly spilling his drink. "Don't say that!"

"What? What did I do?"

"Don't call her a freak. You don't even know her. You don't know anything about her." Carly took a long sip of her icy soda, hoping that it would cool the sudden flash of anger. Why did even nice people like Nick have to do that, labeling kids they had probably never even spoken to as freaks or dorks, nerds and losers.

Nick shrugged his shoulders. "Sorry. It's just that she looks kind of weird and..."

"She's *different*," Carly cut in, "but she's actually pretty nice."

They walked on silently, Carly's anger melting away the closer they got to the ocean. There was barely any breeze off the water tonight, and the air was close and thick. The soda cup had already begun to sweat in the heat and the occasional cold drop felt good as it hit her leg. Nick climbed into the lifeguard stand, and Carly handed the drinks up to him. She pulled herself up into the seat beside him.

"Did you hear about the hurricane?" Nick asked as they sipped their sodas in the darkness.

"Eddie told me. Think it will hit here?"

"They say it might. I don't know, though. Sometimes I think that they make up these predictions just to give the news people something to do, so they can run down here from Philadelphia and film the waves every two hours."

"They *are* huge. I never saw them that big before." Carly and Nick gazed out at the waves. They were crashing against the beach with a relentless fury. Whitecaps glinted way out in the water where the surface was usually smooth.

Nick noisily slurped the last bit of soda from his cup. "You know, I was just thinking. We have a game against Somerville next week, on the field behind the school."

"Yeah?" Carly fished an ice cube from her drink and rubbed it over her forehead and around the back of her neck.

"Yeah, well, I was just wondering if maybe you would like to go. I'm the starting pitcher. I mean, you don't have to or anything if you don't want to."

Carly dropped her hand to her lap and closed it hard around the ice cube. The cool water seeped between her fingers. "I can't," she said simply.

"Okay. No problem. No big deal."

"It's not that I don't want to," Carly added quickly, looking at her lap. She dug her thumbnail up and down the side of the paper cup, scraping off the thin wax coating, trying to fill up the silence that was growing between them. He was probably waiting for her excuse, the good reason why she had to turn him down. But the truth was more uncomfortable than the silence, and she had much more practice with the latter. She worked diligently on the cup and waited.

Nick kept busy with the ice from his soda, scooping out one piece at a time and crunching it between his teeth like popcorn. When the ice was gone, he crumpled the empty cup and squeezed it into a ball shape. He didn't look at her. "It's because your dad doesn't like me, right?" he blurted.

Carly glanced up at him, her face hot with embarrassment.

Nick was gazing out at the water, but he turned to face her. "I mean, he *really* didn't like me. Did I do something wrong or what?"

Carly took a long drink, her cup collapsing under her grip. "No. It's not you," she answered slowly, desperately trying to think of some kind of rational explanation for her father's behavior. But there wasn't one.

"He practically attacked me!"

Carly's heart was pounding with the ferocity of the waves. She had to come up with something. A picture popped into her head. "Well, he didn't like the other five guys who came looking for me this morning,

140

either," she complained. "Actually, he treated you pretty well. The guy before you, my dad shoved him out the door so hard that he flipped over a car and landed in the street. And the one before that? His shirt was ripped from..."

She stopped when she noticed the way Nick was staring at her, his mouth half open.

"I'm kidding, Nick."

"Oh. Yeah. I knew that."

Carly squirmed in her seat, the hard wooden stand suddenly biting into her back and legs. "He'd never let me go," she finally admitted. "I can't really explain it to you. But anyway, even if he would let me, I couldn't go anyway because... because we're moving."

"Moving! No way! When?"

"I don't know. I just know that it's going to be soon."

"Where are you moving to?"

"I don't know."

"Did your dad get a new job or something?"

Carly leaned her head back against the stand. "I don't know that, either. They don't tell me anything. I just get packed up like the rest of the furniture and put down in some new place." Carly was surprised to hear the bitterness leaking out of her voice. Perhaps it was because she had never minded the moves as much before. She had never had this much to lose.

Carly closed her eyes and took a deep breath of the salt air, holding it in her lungs. She wished that there was a way to save it as a souvenir of her summer of freedom.

Nick leaned forward and cleared his throat. "Carly. Don't get mad at me or anything, but I think something really weird is going on here."

She turned to him. "What do you mean?"

"Well, you got this tall man following you around and asking you questions about your dad. And he probably is a Secret Service agent. He doesn't look sinister or creepy."

Carly thought of the man's easy manner when he bought the paper from Eddie tonight, his smile as he joked about the sand Nick had thrown in his face.

"So?" Carly asked.

"So then all of a sudden you're going to pack up and move, and you don't even know where you're going?"

Carly thought of their other moves. Had they been just as quick? There had been so many that the cities and the circumstances seemed to blur together. She couldn't sort them out and she had been too young to care.

"What if your dad is doing something illegal? You can't just move away with him."

"He's not doing anything illegal!" Carly snapped, her voice rising. "Don't you think I would have noticed if he were?" Carly's mind was racing. There was a wall she had built in her head behind which she had stuffed all those unanswered questions and little pieces of things that she had seen or heard in her house that didn't quite fit or make sense. She had kept them back there, out of the way, unexplored. But now, Nick was chipping away at that wall.

"I guess you're right," Nick said quietly.

"I know I am." Carly answered a little too loudly, then bit down hard on the end of her straw.

"Okay. You're right." Nick juggled his soda cup ball back and forth from hand to hand. "But what if..." He stole a quick glance at Carly and almost dropped the ball. "What if, just to be sure before you go, you talk to the tall man and answer his questions. Maybe that would clear this whole thing up. Then you wouldn't have to worry about it."

"I'm not worried about it!" Carly slammed her cup down on the seat between them. "You're the only one who's worried about it!"

"Okay. I'm sorry," Nick said quickly. "It's just that the tall man was in talking to my mom tonight, before I saw you on the boardwalk."

"Oh, great." Carly drew her knees up to her chest. "So now I guess everybody thinks my dad's a criminal."

Nick squeezed the misshapen ball between his palms. "They're just questions," he said.

Carly remembered Margo's questioning eyes burning into her own and she ran her hand over the bandaged cheek. "Your mom was real nice tonight."

Nick smiled. "For some crazy reason, she really likes you."

Carly pulled at the sticky edges of the bandage. "She hardly knows me. I don't know why she likes me."

"Yeah. Me neither." Nick punched her in the arm. "Hey! Come on. I got a great idea!" He jumped down from the lifeguard stand.

"Where are you going?" Carly jumped down beside him.

"You can't go to the game against Somerville next week, right?"

"Yeah?"

"Let's go now, then. To the field, I mean. I could show you around, give you the play-by-play of what I'm going to do." Nick was punching his right hand into his left, as though he had his glove on and the game was about to begin. "I want to strike out at least one batter per inning. I can do it too."

Carly shook her head. "I can't go. The school's too far."

"No it's not. It's only about fifteen or twenty blocks from here. We can take the bus."

"No way," Carly insisted. "I'm not allowed to stay out late."

"But it's early!" Nick made a futile attempt to read his watch in the dark. "What time do you have to be in?"

Carly hesitated. "Just not too late."

"Come on. It'll be fun. What do you have to lose?"

Only an arm or a leg, Carly thought, or the skin on the other side of my face.

Nick didn't wait for an answer. He took her hand in his and started walking. She felt his warm fingers pressed against hers and knew she wouldn't pull away even if they were walking off the end of the pier into the black ocean.

# CHAPTER 17

Carly picked a window seat toward the back of the bus and Nick slipped into the seat beside her. She pushed the window up as far as it would go and let the warm salt air wash over her as the bus rumbled down Atlantic Avenue. Carly stuck her arm out the window and tried to hold it straight against the rushing air.

"I hope Eddie's okay," she said, recalling his stricken face, his magazines strewn about the boardwalk.

"I'm sure he's okay," Nick replied. "Frankie's not the first little jerk to pull a stunt like that. Eddie can take care of himself."

"Did you know that Eddie has a son?" Carly asked.

Nick cracked the gum in his mouth. "No."

"He does. He's our age and he lives in Oceanside."

"No way." Nick took off his baseball cap and ran his hand back through his short hair. "That can't be true."

Carly drew her arm into the bus. "What do you mean?"

"He might visit Oceanside, but he sure doesn't live here."

"How do you know?"

"Because I've lived in Oceanside my whole life. When the shoobies are gone, it's a pretty small place. I mean, we only had one elementary school and I knew every kid in it. I don't remember any kid with the last name Shelengoski. Besides, I never saw Eddie with any kid. What makes you think he's got a son, anyway?"

"He told me. But the weird thing is, the kid doesn't know that Eddie is his father. I bet he has a different last name than Eddie."

Nick ran his hand along the brim of his hat. "Come to think of it, Eddie does go to a lot of our ball games. I just figured it was because he was lonely and had nothing else to do. Who do you think it could be?"

"I don't know. You would know better than me. Is there anybody who lives just with his mom?"

"Sure. Justin Reville, Zack Kane, Andy Turcelli, just to name a few." Nick gave Carly a sideways glance. "And me, of course."

"Do you think any of them look like Eddie?"

"Yeah, right." Nick hunched up his shoulders and puffed out his cheeks with air.

"That's mean!" Carly popped his swollen face with her index finger.

"Carly, come on, nobody looks like Eddie."

The bus rolled to a stop at a small intersection, giving out a loud *shushsh* like a tired sigh of relief, and two teenage girls and one older man boarded, dropping their coins with a rattle into the metal box by the driver.

"Where did the word shoobie come from anyway?" Carly asked as the bus groaned, building speed.

"My mom says that in the old days when the train ran down here from Philly, people used to come to the shore for the day and bring their lunches in shoeboxes. So people started to call them 'shoobies' and it just sort of stuck to all the tourists."

"I think it sounds like a fish. I caught two shad and one shoobie."

Nick laughed. "I always thought it sounded like a word in one of those old songs." He began to sing loudly in a high voice. *"Shoobie doobie do, be doobie doobie."*

Some of the people on the bus turned around to stare at them, and Carly shrunk down in her seat and doubled over in quiet laughter. But Nick was not intimidated.

*"Strangers in the night, be shoobie doobie,"* he crooned.

"Will you stop!?" Carly laughed.

"What's the matter, don't you think I have a good voice?" Nick put his hands over his heart and screwed up his face in mock anguish.

"No," Carly said. "You definitely don't have a good voice."

"Well, thanks a lot." Nick swatted her in the head with his baseball cap.

"Besides," Carly continued, straightening up, "everybody's looking at us. What if I'm being followed again?" She wrapped her hand around the armrest and stared at the backs of the heads of the other passengers.

"Hey, the tall man's head would hit the ceiling in this

147

old bus. He isn't here. Relax. Is there anybody else you're worried about?"

"Aren't we supposed to get off here?" Carly asked.

Nick bolted from his seat. "Yeah, this is it."

Carly held her breath as the bus pulled away, leaving them in a cloud of diesel fumes. "Let's run," she suggested when the air cleared. The school was still about three blocks away.

"Are you kidding?"

"No, I mean it." Sneaking out to the boardwalk was one thing. But the school was much farther from home and being here felt dangerous. Nervousness tingled through her body and she needed to run.

"But it's way too hot," Nick protested.

Carly gave him a half smile. "You're just scared I'm going to beat you."

"Yeah, right. You wouldn't have a chance. But..."

Carly took off before he could finish and he quickly followed. They said nothing, each one pushing hard, trying to stay in front. Carly was almost half a block ahead when Nick stopped and called her back.

"Man, you oughta join the track team," he panted, doubled over on the sidewalk, his hands on his knees. "Of course, the only reason I didn't win was because my ankle's so sore." He walked around her in a circle, doing a fake limp.

Carly crossed her arms on her chest and watched him. "Give it up, Nick," she said.

He straightened up and smiled. "Come on. I'll show you what I'm really good at."

They went past the school to the small baseball field spread out neatly behind it. Nick pushed open the gate in the chain link fence, and it clanked shut behind them. It was fairly dark. The field was lit only by the streetlights that ran up the right field line. Nick stood up on the mound. He rubbed some of the red dirt between his palms and went into his windup. "Steee-riiiike three!" he yelled, as the pebble he had thrown went skidding across the plate.

Carly shook her head.

"I wish you could see the real thing," he said wistfully. "Did you know I pitched my first shutout here? I was real good. I'm going to do it again on Wednesday."

"What's the name of the team you're playing?" Carly asked.

"The Somerville Pirates."

"And who's their best hitter?"

"George Church, no doubt about it."

Carly picked up an old board that was sitting in front of the dugout and stood over home plate. "Okay. Pretend I'm George."

Nick laughed, but he went into his windup and threw a pebble toward the plate. Carly swung her stubby piece of wood.

"Steee-rike one!" Nick yelled.

"I think that was a ball," Carly complained.

"It can't be a ball. You swung at it!"

"Well, I mean if I hadn't swung at it, it would've been a ball. Just make sure you don't hit me."

"It was a perfect pitch. Here comes another one."

149

Nick reached back and threw again. "Steee-rike two!" he yelled.

"What!?" Carly burst out laughing. "I never even saw it! Use a bigger rock this time."

Nick searched the infield and came back to the mound with a rock. "Ladies and gentlemen," he intoned. "It is the bottom of the ninth inning. The Pirates are down one to nothing. There are two outs and the count is three and two. This pitch will decide it all. This pitch..."

"Will you just throw it!" Carly shouted.

Nick hurled the rock toward the plate and Carly swung her makeshift bat. There was a dull cracking noise as the rock hit the wood.

"I hit it! I hit it!" she yelled and raced toward first base.

Nick stood, momentarily stunned. As Carly headed toward second, he ran around the infield and searched for the rock. "No fair! It's too dark. I can't find it!"

Carly was rounding third when Nick stumbled over the rock. He raced after her toward the plate.

"Oh no, oh no," Carly laughed. She had never done it before, but she felt her legs go out in front of her and her feet reach for the plate in a perfect slide. Nick tumbled after her and they lay, tangled and laughing, on home plate. His leg was across her stomach, her head on his shoulder. She lay there, blissfully, breathing in the smell of the damp grass and the fine dirt, staring out past the overhanging chain-link fence to the wide-open sky when something caught the corner of her eye.

She sat up. A dark figure was moving through the stands in left field.

"Nick," she whispered, jumping to her feet. "There's somebody out there."

"Where?"

"In the stands."

"So? It's a public place. It's probably just one of my fans."

Carly squinted in the darkness, then let out a long breath and sat down right on home plate. "It's definitely not one of your fans." Their eyes followed a teenage boy and girl as they climbed out of the stands and left the field, the fence gate clanking behind them. "I think we intruded on their privacy," Carly laughed.

Nick shrugged. They both stood and brushed the dirt off their clothes. They walked past the third baseline, deeper into the darkness, and sat in the grass with their backs against the chain-link fence.

Carly sighed. "I can't believe I have to move from here."

Nick plucked a handful of grass. "Maybe you won't have to."

"I will," Carly said. "It always happens when..." There was something in the way that Nick was avoiding her eyes that made her stop. "What do you mean that maybe I won't have to?"

Nick just shrugged.

Carly shoved him in the shoulder. "Tell me."

"It's nothing."

"Then just tell me." She grabbed his cap.

Nick plucked another handful of grass and let the blades slowly fall through his fingers. "Remember I told you that the tall man was in the pizza shop tonight?"

"Yeah."

"Well, your dad's obviously in some kind of trouble, Carly. You might have to stay around until, you know, it gets cleared up or something."

Carly jumped up. "Can't you just drop it? He isn't in any trouble!"

"How can you just pretend that nothing's happening?" Nick stood in front of her, inches away. "Don't you want to know if your dad's doing something wrong or not?"

She didn't want to know. It was easier not knowing. She shook her head and turned from him.

"How can you be like that? Are you going to spend your whole life wondering if somebody's following you around?"

Carly shrugged. "I'm going to be moving soon, and then I won't have to worry about it anymore."

"Oh right. They're just going to leave you alone because you move to a different state." Nick grabbed his baseball cap out of her hands. "That's stupid."

Carly wondered what had happened at the pizza shop tonight, what Nick had told the tall man about her. Maybe Nick had agreed to play detective and get whatever information he could from her.

"Why do you even care what my father does?" Carly asked, the sharp edge in her voice cutting through the air between them. "Why can't you just forget about it?"

"I just..." Nick's mouth hung open. "I don't know. I just don't think that you should move away with your dad if he's...you know...if he's a criminal or anything."

Carly opened her mouth to protest, but Nick hurried on. "You could get hurt or get in trouble or something. And besides, if you move away, you'll never get to see me pitch!" A small smile played at the corners of his mouth. "And you'd live to regret that, because I'm going to be really famous someday. And not only that..." Nick paused and looked down at his feet. "We were just starting to sort of hang out together, and, if you leave, we wouldn't get to do that anymore."

Carly felt a spreading warmth in her chest, like hot chocolate gulped on a cold day.

"And if you just moved away, I wouldn't even know what happened to you," Nick added quickly. "I mean, I don't want you to take this the wrong way or anything, but, you know, your dad didn't strike me as being the nicest guy in the world." He shot a quick glance at Carly.

"You don't know him," Carly argued. But Nick was getting close, and it was making her nervous.

"Yeah, I know. You're right. It's just that, since this morning, what happened in the candy shop, I wondered a couple of times about that bruise on your face."

Carly winced. She could tell by the way her vision was affected that the eye was now swollen partly shut. The throbbing pain in her face spread to her chest. "I walked into the door! I told you that. You think I'm lying?"

153

Nick opened his mouth, but nothing came out. Carly backed away from him. "I'm leaving." She turned and headed for the gate.

Nick was right at her heels. "Hey, Carly! Listen, I didn't want to make you mad or anything. I just wanted to make sure that it wasn't because of me, that it wasn't my fault."

His hands were stuffed deep in his pockets and his shoulders were hunched up high. Carly let out a deep breath. How could she be mad at him for suspecting the truth, for talking about the thing that everyone else turned away from and pretended they didn't see?

"It's okay," Carly assured him, as Nick fell in step with her. "You didn't do anything. But I *don't* want to talk about this anymore."

But Nick didn't know when to quit. "My dad used to be a police officer, and he said that he thought..."

Carly whirled around. "You talked to your dad about this too?! I thought he didn't live with you."

"He doesn't, but I still talk to him on the phone, and he visits a lot."

"What exactly did you tell him about me?"

"I didn't use your name or anything. Well, maybe your first name," Nick stuttered. "Anyway, I think I might have just told him I was asking because it was for a school project on crime prevention or something."

Carly turned and strode off the field, slamming the gate in Nick's face.

# CHAPTER 18

"Come on," Nick complained. "I don't know what you're so upset about. You're acting like a baby."

Carly leaned her head against the bus window and stared out at the darkness. A light rain had begun to fall and the drops slowly streaked past her eyes and down the grimy glass. The air inside the bus was warm and sticky and smelled of sweat and old seat cushions. The lights were dim. She curled closer to the window.

"Well, fine, then," Nick growled. "Be that way." He kicked the seat in front of him and slouched down, his baseball cap pulled low over his eyes.

What was there to talk about, anyway? Carly pulled her silence around her and held it tightly. It was like the security blanket, warm and soft and familiar, that she had never had. When she was under it, she felt safe and protected. Now Nick was pulling up the edges, trying to see in. He was questioning her bruise and wondering aloud about her family. Of all the people in the world, he was the one she could never let see.

When the bus stopped at 31$^{st}$ Street, Carly bounded

down the steps and headed up the dark street in the rain. Nick fell in step beside her.

"I'll walk you home," he offered, his hands in his pockets.

"No." She began to walk faster.

"I'll just follow you then."

Carly stopped and wheeled around to face him. "I don't want to be followed anymore—by *anyone*."

"Okay, okay. Follow was the wrong word. I'll just make sure you get in okay."

"No." The rain was falling harder now, hitting her in the face and running down her neck. She had to get in, but she couldn't let Nick see her crawl in the window. She began to walk again.

Nick was at her shoulder. "Look, what did I do that was so wrong? I didn't give anything away to my dad."

"Oh, right." Carly paused under a tree. "A summer project on crime prevention? Give me a break. Your dad didn't have to be a detective to figure out that that was bogus. Just go home, okay?"

"It's a free country," Nick retorted. "I can walk down this street if I feel like it."

The wind had picked up and the rain was lashing against Carly's legs, the drops hitting the sidewalk like tiny grenades, exploding on impact. She could think of no good reason Nick would hang around in weather like this. "What are you doing, working for the Secret Service agents now, helping them out by following me around?"

"I was trying to help *you*," Nick shouted into the wind.

"Well, forget it. I can take care of myself." Carly

began to run. "Go away and leave me alone," she called over her shoulder.

Carly ran three blocks without stopping, then ducked behind a parked car. The rain on the hood was like an insistent drumbeat, and it echoed inside her chest. She peeked up the street. She couldn't see Nick. She sat on the curb and took off her shoes and socks. The shoes were still gritty with sand and she sat them in the stream of water that ran down the curb toward the gutter. She rinsed the sand from her feet and carefully peeled the bandage from her wet face. She dropped it and watched as the water grabbed it, a white rudderless boat, and carried it along in the current, finally sucking it into the sewer hole at the corner.

She stood across the street from her house, behind the oak tree, her body pressed against the warm bark. The house was dark, but this gave her no comfort. If he knew she was out, he would probably wait for her in the dark, purposeful, pacing like a cat, tensing at the first sound of her arrival.

Carly crossed the street and crept into the backyard. The old maple tree was groaning in the wind, beating itself against the house as though it wanted to be let in, out of the storm. The leaves and branches lashed her in the face and arms as she tried to climb. She fell hard to the ground once but managed to make it to the roof on her second try. She inched across the roof on her hands and knees, gripping the wet tiles and leaning into the wall, bracing herself against the gusts that threatened to push her over the edge.

She finally reached the window and clung to the ledge. The peeling paint came loose in her hands and she wiped it against the side of the house. The rain was falling so hard that it stung her arms and legs and plastered her hair across her face. She wedged her fingers in the small crack under the window and pushed, but it wouldn't budge. The wood must have swollen in the dampness. She struggled to her feet, clinging to the frame. She worked at the window from the top, pushing, pulling, wiggling it open just wide enough that she was finally able to squeeze herself through, stifling a cry as her swollen cheek scraped against the sill. She stood panting, just inside the room, dripping, listening. The air was close and still. The rain thundered against the house. She squinted in the darkness, but couldn't make out his form anywhere in the room. She strained to hear his breathing or for any slight movement, but there was nothing.

Other than the puddle that was growing at her feet, her room seemed just as she had left it. She switched on the light and was momentarily blinded. Her eyes darted to the door. She squinted and blinked. The tape still stretched across the frame. Nothing was disturbed. He hadn't even come in her room.

Carly flopped back on the bed and let out a long breath toward the ceiling that made the cobwebs dance in the corner. She peeled off her wet clothes and pulled on an oversized T-shirt. She sat cross-legged on her bed in front of the fan watching the door, brushing the wet from her hair. It was 11:30. The whole room seemed to be wet, filled with steam from the rising storm, and there was nowhere she could let it out. She stood and went to the window, trying to see out through the driving rain. Shadows danced all around the yard, shimmered and blurred near the neighbors' porch lights, whirled around the blowing trees. She left the window open just as it was when she had crawled in and stuffed a towel in the crack. She couldn't bear to force it closed and seal herself in. Her eyes searched the yard again. Maybe she was just being paranoid, but she couldn't help feeling that someone was there, watching. She shut off her light and sat on the bed, brushing, brushing.

# CHAPTER 19

There was a sudden loud crack, like a snapping whip, then a slow groan. Carly sat up, still half asleep, the brush stuck in her hair. "I didn't..." she mumbled, twisting around in the darkness. A thunderous crash shook her room, and something huge scraped past the window. Carly jumped up, the pillow clutched to her chest. The rain was thrumming against the house, and the wind pushed at the walls, moaning and whistling. Somewhere below, a door slammed. A weak pool of light spilled under her door. Carly quickly grabbed her wet clothes and threw them under the bed. She ran her hands through her hair. It was still damp, but so was everything in her room. There was a faint knocking on the door.

"Carly, Carly," Mrs. Chambers hissed "Are you okay?"

Carly cracked opened the door. Her mother stood in the hallway, trembling, wrapped in an old robe, her hair disheveled from sleep.

"I'm fine," Carly answered, gazing down the hall. "What happened?"

Mrs. Chambers moved across the room to the small window. Her hand gripped the sill. "The tree," she said simply. "It's the tree."

Carly gazed out the window. A weak light played about in the yard, her father with a flashlight. The small beam moved through the rain and the darkness and Carly saw. The tree had split, its huge graceful branches piled heavily in the wet yard. It lay weakly waving its uppermost limbs, like a beached whale straining futilely to rise. The flashlight trailed up the scarred trunk to the few branches that remained aloft, swooning around, exposed and alone.

Suddenly the light flashed up to their window. Mrs. Chambers shrank back into the darkness. Carly squinted. Was he only checking to see if she was okay, or did he somehow suspect her recent presence in the ruined tree? Like a mole, he could often sense what he could not see, burrowing into her life, uncovering secrets, clipping the roots of her carefully laid plans. A tremor ran down her spine.

"What happened with your window?"

Carly fingered the wet towel stuffed into the opening. "Nothing. It was hard to shut so I just put this in here."

Mrs. Chambers nodded and turned to leave, but Carly grabbed her mother's hand. It was cool, a collection of small bones covered with thin, slippery skin that felt as though it would crumble to nothing if she squeezed too hard. "Stay with me for a little bit," she begged.

Her mother hesitated, her back against the wall.

"Please?" Carly asked, pulling her toward the bed. "Couldn't you sit here, just for a little bit? I'll close the door," she offered.

"No," Mrs. Chambers whispered. "Leave it open, so I can listen." She moved to the bed and sat beside Carly, shoulders hunched, facing the door, her face weakly lit by the light from the hallway. It was a fallen face, melted almost, like the Santa candle she sat too close to the stove, his jolly smile and whiskers all drooping into a small wax puddle. Carly tried to re-form her mother's profile, imagining how she had looked as a young woman, as a bride. They had no photographs hanging in their house, no albums tucked away in drawers. Their family history lived somewhere in the silences that filled their mealtimes and behind dark eyes that always looked away.

Carly squeezed her mother's hand, felt the skin slide back over the small bones. "How old were you when you got married?" she asked, digging for details to fill out the picture she was sketching in her head.

Mrs. Chambers pulled her hand away. "What brought that up?"

Carly shrugged. "I don't know. I just wondered."

"Too young," her mother answered. "That's all. Just too young."

"What was it like?"

Mrs. Chambers stood and began to fiddle with the things on top of Carly's dresser, straightening and rearranging the brush and comb and hair bands. "Cold," she mumbled. "It was a cold day."

"That's not what I mean."

Mrs. Chambers moved to the window and adjusted the towel stuck in the opening. Carly followed her. "I mean, what was your wedding gown like? Was it a big wedding in a church? Who was there?"

Mrs. Chambers sighed and bit her lower lip.

"Well? What was it like? Can't you tell me? Do you have any pictures?"

Her mother's hands went still and she stared at the blank wall.

"Do you?" Carly repeated. She searched her mother's face for any trace of the girl who once was.

"No," her mother said quietly. "There's nothing, nothing at all."

"Oh." Carly's shoulders slumped. Her mother started toward the door, but Carly grabbed her shirt. "Then tell me about when I was born."

Her mother's face softened and lifted at the edges and around the eyes. "I've told you that story before."

"I know, but not in a long time."

Mrs. Chambers took Carly's hand between her own two. "You were so tiny and sweet. Your fingers," she remembered, holding up Carly's hand, "were so small, with little pink fingernails no bigger than drops of water. Look at them now." She placed Carly's palm flat against her own. "They're bigger than mine!"

Carly folded her fingers into her mother's.

"You were the most beautiful baby in the nursery, so delicate. And it wasn't just me saying that. All the nurses thought so too. That little tuft of brown hair, those big blue eyes that filled up half your face. I remember when I nursed you, you always wrapped your fist around my finger and held tight."

"What about Dad?" Carly asked. "Did he ever, you know, hold me and stuff like that?"

Her mother's back stiffened. "He didn't understand

babies. He didn't know what to do. He was confused and then...and then it made him so angry sometimes." A small smile played across her face. "You cried a lot, you know. Kept us awake at night."

Carly pulled on the ends of her hair. "But that wasn't my fault! Babies do that!"

Mrs. Chambers ran her hand down Carly's arm. "Of course it wasn't your fault."

Carly pushed back on the bed. "But he's still angry—about everything I do." She fingered her still sore face. "All I said yesterday was I didn't want to move. What's so wrong with that? Why can't we just stay in Oceanside?"

Mrs. Chambers hung her head and let out a deep breath. "We have to go," she said simply. Then she looked up. "There are things that we should talk about, Carly. Things I should probably tell you. I've wanted to talk to you for so long, to explain. It's just that there never seems to be a good time. And I worry that your father..."

There was a slam downstairs, the back door thrown shut. Mrs. Chambers jumped, electrified as though touched by the lightening from the storm. "I have to go," she said.

"But wait!" Carly grabbed the back of her mother's shirt again, holding her in the doorway.

"We'll find a good time to talk," her mother whispered. "Soon."

Carly tightened her grasp. "When?"

"As soon as we can. Now let go," she urged. "This will only cause more trouble."

Carly stamped her foot. "Why can't you stay? Why?"

She knew the answer, but it wasn't fair.

"Because I can't," Mrs. Chambers hissed. "We'll talk later."

"I want to talk now!" Carly demanded, her voice rising. "I want to know when we're moving. I want to know where we're going. I want to..."

Mrs. Chambers slapped her cool hand over Carly's mouth and took a quick look down the hall. "In the next few days," she said softly.

"I don't want to go!" Carly pouted. "Can't we just let him go without us?"

Mrs. Chambers pulled Carly back into the room and sat her on the bed, her hands tightening on Carly's shoulders. "Don't ever say such a thing," she snapped. "Where would we be without him? What would we do? Live on the street? Is that what you want?"

Mrs. Chambers gently ran her hand down the swollen bruise on Carly's face. "It will get better," she said. "Things will be better in our new home. You'll see. And we'll talk. As soon as..."

"Leila!" Mr. Chambers' voice boomed up the stairs.

Mrs. Chambers jerked away from Carly's bed. "He needs dry clothes," she explained. "I have to go. Maybe I'll come back later," she whispered, disappearing silently from the room.

"Yeah, maybe," Carly muttered to the blank ceiling. She felt a sudden burning hate for the "maybe game." It was nothing but wait, go back three spaces, lose all your turns. She had no chance of ever winning.

Carly lay heavily on her bed, the heat pressing against

her chest, pinning her to the blankets, the rain falling in sheets above her. In this box of a room she felt like she was lying in a coffin, lid closed, and the dirt was raining down around her, filling up the hole that used to be her life. She had a few days left, but what did it matter now? The tree was down. There was no way to get out. Even if the storm let up, she would never see the boardwalk again or get to say good-bye to Eddie or Margo or Angela. Or Nick. She had fought with him and told him to leave her alone. Her last hour with him she'd spent staring out a bus window, then stalking away, refusing to talk. She'd never get to undo that now. He'd probably forget about her quickly. She'd become a distant memory, the weird girl he had felt sorry for that summer when he was thirteen. Carly felt as if something had broken inside her. Like a crushed shell, the sharp-edged pieces were sticking painfully in her chest and throat.

There was a faint clicking noise and then the fan died, the blades taking a few final slow turns. The light disappeared from under her door. Carly pulled herself from bed and peered out the window. The whole town was dark. The electricity was out as far as she could see.

She tried to make out the tree, but it was swallowed up by the darkness of the storm. She felt guilty somehow, almost as though her furtive use of the tree had turned it into an accomplice and it had suffered in her place. She was glad she wouldn't be around to watch the gradual wilting of its graceful branches, the leaves slowly starving, curling from soft green to brittle brown.

Carly collapsed on her bed in the darkness, damp with

sweat, and listened to the storm rage around the house. She couldn't sleep. Her mind was filled with thoughts of Nick and Eddie and what the "things" were that her mother had wanted to tell her.

Finally, there was a clanging of pots and pans in the kitchen and she realized that it must be near morning. She slipped on a dry pair of shorts and a clean T-shirt and crept downstairs. The kitchen was a few degrees cooler than her bedroom, but the air was still thick and heavy with heat. A small candle burned on the table.

"Good morning, love." Mrs. Chambers reached quickly into the dark refrigerator and pulled out the carton of eggs. "Can I make you something?"

"No, thanks." Carly slipped into one of the chairs. "It's too hot to eat."

A blue flame shot up from the range and the strips of bacon began to sizzle. "How long is this storm supposed to last?" Carly asked. "Is it a real hurricane?"

"It was a hurricane—Hurricane Annie—but now it's been downgraded to a tropical storm. They never know these things for sure, but it's supposed to let up tonight." Mrs. Chambers used the back of her arm to brush the hair out of her eyes and she flipped the bacon.

Carly played with the salt and pepper shakers, clinking them together and moving them apart. "Do you think if the storm stops tomorrow, then me and you, we could take a quick walk to the beach or something? You know, just to talk like you said we could." Carly ran the salt down the crack in the table.

Mrs. Chambers turned suddenly, her eyes wide, the

fork suspended in midair. "No, no, no." She took a quick look down the hallway. "There is too much to do these next few days."

"But, I want to know about..."

The floorboards creaked down the hall as her father made his way toward the smell of the frying bacon. Mrs. Chambers quickly turned back to the stove, lowering the flame. She pulled plates and utensils from the cabinet.

"I'll be down in the store, sweeping up or something," Carly grumbled. She knew her father would send her down anyway. The bruise on her face, now turning deep shades of purple and blue, would anger him, as though she wore it purposely as a bold rebuke to his actions.

Carly walked slowly down the back stairs into the shop. Water was seeping under the shop door, and she grabbed an old towel from behind the counter and stuffed it around the bottom of the frame. She stood and gazed into the deserted street, amazed at the amount of rain falling from the sky. The sewer was backed up and the water was inching over the curbs. The traffic lights were dark without electricity and swayed perilously on their wires. But it didn't matter. No cars approached the intersection from either direction. A plastic lawn chair tumbled down the street in the wind and Carly noticed several overturned trash cans wedged under cars and behind bushes. Even the storms here were fun to watch.

Carly heard a noise on the stairs behind her and turned to find her father with a box in his hand and a strange look on his face.

# Chapter 20

"Vinnie, no." Mrs. Chambers moved quickly into the shop, her left hand gripping the side wall, her right hand across her stomach.

"It has to be done," he said, striding toward Carly.

"But look at that storm! Can't it wait until tomorrow?" Mrs. Chambers ran up behind him and slipped her hands around his thick arm. "She's just a little girl! She can't go out in that, she could get hurt. Let me go instead."

"Forget it. You can't go in your condition. You wouldn't make it one block." Mr. Chambers shook his wife off his arm and handed the package to Carly. "This goes to the Pacific Avenue address. You know which one I mean, or do I have to write it down for you?"

Carly's mouth hung open and she looked away from him out into the storm.

Mr. Chambers grabbed a pad and pencil and shook his head. "You'd forget your name if I didn't remind you of it every day." He leaned on the counter and scribbled the address that Carly knew well onto a scrap of paper.

"Here." He thrust it into her hand. "Now go."

"Vinnie, please, can't we wait till it calms down?"

"It's not that bad yet. It's just a heavy rain. She won't melt. Besides, I just heard on the radio that it might get a lot worse later on. It might come close to hitting us and then we'll have to get out quickly. You know it has to be delivered. Don't be stupid."

"But, Vinnie, what difference will one day make?" Mrs. Chambers clung to his arm, her hands climbing up toward his shoulder with each word. "She can go tomorrow, we can wait to leave until..."

Mr. Chambers flung his arm back violently to shake his wife off, his elbow catching her in the neck. She lost her grip on him and fell backward, her head hitting the display case. Her body slid to the floor.

"Mom!" Carly jumped toward her mother but her father grabbed her arm, pulling her back, his fingers pinching painfully into her skin.

"Now look what you've done!" he thundered at Carly, shaking her hard. His hair was damp with perspiration and beads of sweat rolled down the sides of his face and darkened his shirt collar. "None of this would have to happen if you would just . . . *Do . . . What . . . You're . . . Told!*"

Her head snapped back with his last violent jerk on her arm and she felt something break, not a bone or a blood vessel, but it was as though a wall inside her had crumbled and the winds of the hurricane came roaring in. She glared at him and set her jaw. She wrenched her arm free. Fists clenched, she backed away, watching him through narrowed eyes, her breath coming hard and fast. He turned away and lowered his head, banging both fists hard on the counter. Carly dropped beside her mother. "Are you okay?" she panted.

Mrs. Chambers clasped Carly's hand and raised herself to a sitting position. "It's okay, it's okay," she said in a weak voice. "I just, I slipped on the wet floor is all."

Carly saw a streak of red on the display case and slid her hand behind her mother's head. It felt wet and sticky. Her mother winced.

"You're bleeding!" Carly cried. "Don't move! Let me get..."

But her words were cut short. Mr. Chambers grabbed Carly by the hair and pulled her to her feet. "She doesn't need your help," he hissed in her ear. "All you ever do is cause her grief." His fist still gripping her hair, he pulled her toward the door. She could do nothing but follow him, squinting with the pain of her scalp pulled tight.

"I'll take care of your mother. You get that package delivered and get back here." He opened the door and shoved her out. "And, Carly!" he called to her through the noise of the driving rain. "Be careful out there." Then he shut the door.

She stood disbelieving, the rain pelting her back. She was drenched in less than a minute. Waves of water were falling from the sky, pushed by the wind, and they fell over her. She waded through the ankle-deep puddle that was forming in front of the store and stopped just past the display window, flattening herself against the wall. She peeked back into the shop. Her mother was still on the floor, but he was sitting beside her, his arm supporting her narrow shoulders, his hand stroking her hair. She watched him lean over and kiss her mother's forehead.

Carly turned away. Maybe they would be happier without her, free to care for each other without her constant irritation. Maybe it was all her fault, with her anger and her sullenness. Maybe her mother didn't mind him. Maybe she loved him anyway. Carly had tried loving him. Over and over she tried. And there were some times when she thought she could. The night he had taught her to square dance, swinging her around the small room until she was dizzy with laughter, collapsing on the floor, while he continued to stomp and call out the silly steps. Or the time she had crawled under the car when he was changing the oil, and she had held the can for him while the thick glop dripped from one of those dirty pipes. She came out with black streaks down her arms and oil smeared across her face. He laughed so hard that his own dirty face was streaked with tears. He scooped her up and carried her into the house, carefully washing the oil from her skin and calling her "Carly car mechanic."

But the happy memories were like small, infrequent watering holes in a large expanse of desert. And the older she got, the less she longed for them. But wasn't it unnatural not to love your father? That's what he always said after punishing her and watching the hatred rise in her face. It was why he always had to send her to her room or the closet, to hide away those unnatural looks and smother them with darkness.

Carly shuddered. She felt like flinging the box into the wind and letting it get sucked out to sea. And what would he do then? Whatever precious thing had to be delivered in this storm would be lost to him forever, and he would learn what it felt like to lose what you cared about most.

Something caught her eye and Carly glanced over toward Aileen's house. It wasn't funny at all, but she couldn't help smiling anyway. A white sheet flapped from Aileen's bedroom window. It took Carly a minute to figure it out. It was spray painted in bright blue. She must have worked on it last night before she went to bed. It read, "13 days, 19 hours." Carly thought of Aileen just beyond that wall, sound asleep in oversized pajamas, pierced nose, and wild hair, a modern girl in a Victorian bedroom, and felt a little guilty about tricking her. The sheet was useless. The countdown was a waste of time.

Carly wondered where she would be in 13 days and 19 hours. Not that it really mattered. Wherever it was, she'd be alone again. She clutched the box to her chest and pushed up the street into the storm. There was no need to run today. Her father hadn't set the timer. He couldn't possibly know what the streets were like or how long it would take her to get to the Pacific Avenue address. This wasn't so bad after all. It was better than being at home.

The rain was drenching but warm, and it was something of an adventure to be a part of the storm.

The water rushing down the sidewalks spilled over the tops of her sneakers and ran through her shoes. The little white pebbles that only yesterday had sat so neatly in smooth rectangles in front of the beach homes were now creeping with the flowing water out of their beds and across the sidewalks, exposing the sand below.

One pebble had found its way into Carly's shoe, jamming into her heel or arch with every step. She paused and squinted up the block through the rain, searching. A small blue Cape Cod, two houses away, seemed totally dark, no candlelight flickering from within, no car parked in the driveway. She made her way around to the back looking for the outdoor shower. Every beach house had one. In the late after-noons in summer, you could walk down any street and see the spreading puddles of soapy, sandy water trickling from under these showers.

Carly found what she had hoped for. This shower was enclosed and had a small slanted roof. The rusty hinges squealed as she opened the door. She slipped inside and slid the latch shut. An old striped bathing suit hung on a plastic hook, dripping and swaying in the wind. Though the shower was enclosed, there was a gap of several inches between the floor and the bottom walls, and between the roof and the top walls. Carly moved a sticky bar of soap and a half empty shampoo bottle aside and sat on the little wooden bench. She fished the pebble from her shoe.

The rain drummed against the side of the shower and she sat, listening to it, staring at the package on her lap.

How can you not want to know? Nick's words kept playing through her head. Her dripping hair was plastered to her face and she pushed it back, out of her eyes. Slowly she slid the box from the plastic bag her father had wrapped around it. A gust of wind brought a spray of water into the shower and speckled the brown paper wrapper with dark wet spots. Carly sucked in her breath as she watched the stains spread across the paper. It was too late to change her mind.

She turned the package over and slid her finger under a corner of the wrapping. The air was so wet that the tape popped easily wherever she pulled at it. She pushed back the paper and stared at the box. It was a candy box, white with gold lettering, five pounds. She lifted the lid, but there was no smell of chocolate. A thin, white plastic liner with rows of crinkly ridges sat on top. It was used to protect the candy, to keep the pieces safe in their little paper cups.

Carly's fingers were dripping. There was nothing to dry them on. Slowly she lifted the corner of the liner with the very edge of her nails. For a moment, she couldn't breathe. It was money, row after neat row of perfect green bills. And there were two small papers with numbers and dates whose meaning she didn't understand, scribbled in her father's handwriting. Water dripped from the tip of her nose and chin, and several small green pools began to form on the stacks of bills. Carly fit the lid back on and tried to rewrap the box. But the tape wouldn't stick, and the brown paper was wet and mottled. She smoothed it the best she could and shoved it back into the plastic bag. She left the shower and looked around for a deep puddle. There were plenty to pick from, and she dropped the package in a large one down by the curb. She let it sit for a minute, long enough for water to seep into the bag. Her father always ranted about her clumsiness. She'd use it to her advantage for once, claiming that the package was slippery, and she had dropped it in the storm.

Carly continued up 33rd toward Pacific Avenue, oblivious to the storm. The wind pushed at her one way and then another, but she was hardly aware of it. Her mind was filled with green money and long numbers. She floated along through the rain and rising water until she stood in front of the Pacific Avenue house. A plastic chair sat overturned by the front door, and it scraped along the wooden porch with the wind.

The man who lived here was middle-aged, with a full beard and thinning brown hair. He rarely spoke when Carly made her deliveries, only opened the door, cigarette dangling from the corner of his mouth, and nervously snatched the packages from her. Carly climbed the porch steps and knocked lightly on the door. It was opened immediately. He slouched in the doorway in a pair of gray pants and a wrinkled blue shirt, puffing on his cigarette. "Come in, come in," he said, reaching out to grab her arm.

"No, I can't." Carly jumped back out of his reach, and he came out onto the porch.

The gusting winds blew spray into his face, and he squinted at her. "But you're soaking! Come in and dry off.

I'll give you something to drink."

"No. I'm fine," Carly insisted, taking another step back. "I have to get home."

"Not even for a quick snack?" The man took another step toward her. He wasn't wearing any shoes. "How's your father? Do you know when you guys are going to...?"

"Sorry, I gotta go!" Carly backed up all the way to the street.

"Hey! The package!" the man yelled.

Carly stared at the box in her hand. The tall man would love to see this. Her father would die.

"C'mon, kid. What are you doing? Give it to me."

Carly moved behind a car parked at the curb. But wasn't she part of all this too? She'd been making deliveries and turning a blind eye for two years.

The man flicked his cigarette away and bounded down to the car, leaning up against the hood, palms down.

"I want it now," he demanded, smoke trailing out his nostrils. "Stop playing games."

She knew she could outrun him. He wasn't even wearing shoes and had probably smoked cigarettes since he was twelve. But the box felt heavy in her hands, like a time bomb, and she wasn't sure it wouldn't blow up in her face. "Here. Take it," Carly said, quickly handing it off to him. He stared hard at her for a moment, then retreated to the shelter of his porch. "Go on. Get out of here." He tucked the package under one arm and waved her off with the other. "A kid shouldn't be out in a storm like this."

Carly looked up at the low, dark sky and slowly splashed her way up the street.

# Chapter 21

The rain had slowed to a steady drizzle. The streets were still mostly deserted, but here and there people emerged from their homes to sweep back the escaping stones or retrieve an overturned trashcan from a neighbor's lawn. An occasional car braved the flooded streets, moving slowly, like a sputtering motorboat, and leaving a wake behind.

Carly cut across 23rd street to Bell Avenue, which was lined with shops for the tourists. Though she never had any money to spend and rarely any time to linger, she liked to pass the store windows and gaze at all the items on display. Carly stopped in front of an art gallery. A small picture sat in the corner of the window. It was of a lifeguard stand sitting near a dune on an empty beach, facing the green ocean. The sky was lit with pink and pale orange, and the sun was just rising.

She pulled a small piece of paper from her pocket and gazed down at it. She had wrapped it in a plastic baggie and taped it shut, but some water had managed to seep in anyway. Margo's name and telephone number were still clear, but where Carly had written "Nick" all around the edges of the paper, the ink had begun to run.

Carly heard a strange groaning and cracking sound and quickly stuffed the paper back in her pocket. The stores on Bell Avenue all had doors set back in small entryways. The sound was coming from the next store down, a sports card and souvenir shop. She peeked around the corner of the store window. It took her a minute to know what she was looking at. Frankie stood near the door, shoeless and soaking wet, with a bar in his hand. He had splintered the wood near the handle, but the door was still shut tightly.

She turned to run, but she had hesitated a moment too long. Frankie had her by the shirt and pulled her into the alcove.

"Listen, Chambers," he growled. "You open your mouth about this to anyone and I'll bash your skull in. Got it?"

"Get your hands off me," Carly snapped, pulling her shirt free.

He gave her a shove toward the street, then set back to work, sticking the metal bar into the doorjamb and trying to jimmy it open.

Suddenly Frankie stopped and turned toward her, a smile forming at the corner of his lips. "Hey, did you hear about your boyfriend keeling over on the boardwalk last night?"

"What?" Carly's heart fell to the bottom of her stomach. She thought of Nick, wet from the storm, upset by their fight and stricken by . . . by what?

"You heard me. They had to tie him to the top of the ambulance because he was too fat to fit inside. It took twenty men to lift him. I've seen whale rescues that were simpler."

"Eddie!?" she gasped.

"And he whimpered like the..."

She couldn't listen to this. "You're a liar!" she shouted.

Frankie suddenly grabbed Carly by the shirt and shoved her up against the display window. He pinned her shoulders to the glass with his metal bar. "What did you call me?"

Carly had always avoided looking Frankie in the eyes, preferring instead to stare at the ground or her own hands, silently praying that he would leave her alone. But as the bar pinched painfully into her shoulders, she glared at him. His eyes were small and gray and the long curly lashes on his lids did nothing to soften the meanness she saw there.

"You think I'm a liar, huh?" He shoved the bar harder against her. "You know what else they had to do to your fat boyfriend? They..."

Carly felt a wave of anger building inside her and before she even knew what she was doing, it broke. She shoved Frankie off with all her might. He stumbled back against the wall on the other side of the entryway, and she hit him in the face, hard. She had meant it to be a slap, but her fists were clenched and there was a cracking noise as bone hit bone. He was momentarily stunned, and she punched him again. The force of the blow knocked his head against the door, and he slid to the ground. But she didn't stop. She leaned down, preventing him from getting up, and hit him over and over. A cut opened on his face and a trickle of blood ran down his cheek. Carly looked at the back of her hand. It was red. She froze. She saw her face reflected in the glass window, twisted in anger, looking exactly like her father's often did.

Frankie touched his hand to the cut and glanced down at the blood on his fingers. He grabbed the metal bar and struggled to his feet. His eyes were wild, his nostrils flared, like a wounded animal. Carly backed away.

A car horn blared just behind them. Frankie took a swipe at her with the pipe, but she ducked out of the way and he missed.

The car horn blared again. Carly heard the car door click open, but she couldn't afford to take her eyes off Frankie.

"Hey, hey! What's going on there?" came a voice.

Frankie took one more wide swipe at her before running away. "You're dead, Chambers! I swear I'm going to kill you," he screamed, his voice choked with swallowed tears.

"Are you okay?"

Carly turned to see the tall man standing beside her. She tried to answer him, but nothing came out. She nodded and wiped her hand on the back of her shorts, trying to get rid of the red stain.

"Why don't you come sit in my car for a minute? You don't look too good." He rested his long-fingered hand on her shoulder.

The pounding in her chest was painful. She rubbed her hand against her pants over and over, but it was useless. The full moon was coming, and as much as she hated it and no matter how hard she tried, his genes were just too strong. The transformation was starting. She was turning into her father.

"I can't," Carly managed to mutter. "I have to go."

"What was that all about? Who was that kid?"

"Nothing," Carly lied. "Really. It was nothing." She wiped her hand across her shorts again. The wind gusted and lifted her hair out of her face.

The tall man put his hand under her chin and tilted her head back. His eyes were deep blue, like the middle of the ocean, and she was held by them for a moment.

He gently touched the bruise on the side of her face. "How did that happen?"

Carly shrugged and jerked away from him.

But the tall man took her by the shoulders. "Listen, Carly. I know we started off on the wrong foot. I got a little, well, a little overzealous. I just want you to know that I'm on your side, okay?"

Carly nodded, but she knew that they weren't on the same side. He was with the good guys and she was a part of the bad. The pounding in her chest had slowed and she suddenly felt very tired. She wanted to stick her wrists out like they did on television, to confess and let him take her away. But she couldn't. There were things she had to do.

The tall man pulled a business card out of his pocket. "I want you to take this. If you're ever in trouble or you want to tell me something or you just need help, give me a call."

Carly looked down at the name. William Jenkins. United States Department of Treasury. Office number. Cell number. "It'll get wet." She tried to hand it back to him.

He reached into his pocket. "Here. Take a bunch. The card in the middle should stay dry."

It wasn't worth fighting about. She could dump them later. Carly slipped the cards into her wet pocket and wiped her hand again on the back of her pants.

"You better get home," he said before he ducked into his car. "This is just a lull in the storm. It's going to get worse before it gets better."

"Okay," Carly said. But she didn't start for home. There was something she had to do first.

# CHAPTER 22

The rain was only misting down now, and the wind had slowed to an occasional gust. Carly hurried toward the boardwalk. She felt like a fly in a soup bowl. Drenched and sticky, she strained to move quickly through the humid, steaming streets, but the huge puddles and flooded roads grabbed at her legs and forced her to move as if in slow motion.

She finally reached the ramp at 33rd Avenue and rushed up to the boardwalk, her shoes squishing with every step. But at the top of the ramp she stopped dead. She stared at the scene, wide-eyed. Magazines were strewn about the boardwalk, their wet pages flapping helplessly in the wind. Sodden newspapers lay like clumps of beached seaweed, the print from one section bleeding into the next. Stray pages ripped loose by the wind had collected under benches and wrapped themselves around trashcans and storefronts.

Carly dragged herself toward the stand, her heart heavy. Maybe what Frankie had said was true after all. Her stool was gone, blown who knows where by the storm.

The metal display racks were on their sides, up against the wall of the stand. The front window flap was open and the thin door swung on one hinge. Carly collected the wet magazines and piled them in the corner of the stand. She wasn't sure why she did it, no one would ever buy them now. But she just couldn't leave Eddie's things lying all over the boardwalk like that.

She sat on the floor inside the stand, her head in her hands. She thought back to last night, to Eddie's gray face, his anger and sadness at what Frankie and his friends had done. Eddie was probably feeling sick then, but all he was concerned about was the little bit of blood on her face. And she had left him and gone off to the baseball field with Nick, never checking back to make sure he was okay. She had been selfish, thinking of nothing but her own problems.

Something dark sat in a small cubbyhole near the floor of the stand. She reached her hand in and pulled it out. A wallet. The emergency crew probably never saw it. Carly opened it and flipped through the pictures inside, smiling. There was Eddie as a child, standing between his parents in front of a small house, chubby cheeks balanced, like two red balloons, on the tips of an enormous grin. She saw Eddie all dressed up in a tux, dark hair slicked back, at his high school prom.

The next photograph stopped Carly cold. Why would he have such a picture? She flipped back to the front, to the driver's license, to make sure that this was really Eddie's wallet. It was. She turned back to the photo and stared disbelievingly. Frankie's smirking face glared up at

185

her from his school portrait. She inched her fingers into the little plastic cover and pulled out the photo and those that were stuffed behind it. They were all of Frankie, from a baby propped against pillows, to a toddler clutching a Big Bird doll, to a little boy in his first baseball uniform, to...to whatever thing he was now.

She couldn't believe it. Her hand trembling, she slipped Frankie's pictures back into the plastic holder and stuck the wallet in her pocket. She unlatched the wooden board from the ceiling and pulled it down over the opening in the front of the stand, securing the clips at the base. There was no way she could lock the broken door, but she shut it as best she could and shoved a tied bundle of wet papers against it to keep it from blowing open.

Carly ran to Margo's Pizza, the wallet chafing against her thigh, desperate for news about Eddie. The boardwalk was more peopled than the streets inland. Shop owners were taking advantage of the lull in the storm to check their stores and do some additional boarding up. Curious onlookers dotted the oceanside rail here and there, gazing out at the huge, frothy waves pounding ashore. When she got to Margo's, she saw that a metal door had been rolled down and secured across the opening of the pizza shop. No one was there.

Carly reached in her pocket and pulled out the scrap of paper with Margo's telephone number on it. She ran back to Eddie's stand and scoured the ground around it. She picked up some of the loose change that she and Nick had missed last night and ran to the pay phone hanging on the wall outside the Island Breeze clothing shop.

She dropped a quarter into the slot and punched in the number. "Please, please, please answer," she whispered into the receiver as she listened to the phone ring on the other end of the line. At least the phones were working.

"Hi. You have reached 856-752..." Carly kicked the side of the building. No one was home. Just a stupid voicemail system. She gripped the receiver and swallowed a few times waiting for the long beep. She didn't have very much experience talking to these machines.

"Hi. Uh...this is Carly. I'm on the boardwalk and...and I sort of heard a rumor about Eddie being sick. I was just wondering if you knew about it or if you could check on him." She paused and took a deep breath. "And Nick, I wanted to say...that I'm sorry about my getting mad last night and all." Something caught in her throat, painfully, like the tip of a fisherman's hook, and she struggled to pull the last words up. "I probably won't get to see you again. But, you know, thanks for being my friend and all." She dropped the phone into its cradle and fell back against the wall. Water was streaming down her face. She put the heels of her hands over her eyes to make it stop, but it did no good.

She turned and began to run, the water on her face mixing with the rain in the air, the small sobs whisked from her by the wind, their sound smothered in the storm.

Carly stopped in the middle of 31st Street, water lapping around her shins. The wallet. She couldn't take it home with her. It made a noticeable bulge in her pocket and it belonged to Eddie. She couldn't leave it in the stand. It could get ruined. She didn't know anyone to give it to. Panic was building in her chest. A large stone building on the next block caught her eye and she quickly headed for it.

# CHAPTER 23

Holy Innocents Catholic Church sat on the corner of 31st and Ocean Drive, a small apron of green grass neatly bordering its front and sides and a large expanse of blacktop for parking spread out in back. Carly had never been inside. She passed the church many times on her errands, occasionally seeing people flowing out the main doors after mass. The old priest always stood by the door in his long robes, sometimes white, sometimes purple, and warmly shook the hands of the people coming out. Eddie said that he had played Santa Claus here at the Christmas Bazaar. It was the only place she could think of going.

The wind was picking up again, and the rain started to fall heavily. Carly ran up the few steps and grabbed the door handle. She gave several forceful pulls, but it wouldn't budge. Weren't churches always supposed to be open? She hopped back down the steps and sloshed through the puddles to the side door. She grasped the handle and squeezed. It gave a small click and the door opened. Carly slipped quickly inside.

She stood dripping by the door, her mouth open. It was hushed and dark, the only sound the pattering of the rain on the cavernous peaked roof. A faint light drifted through the high stained glass windows, and saints with peaceful faces gazed down on the rows of polished wooden pews. Carly felt the silence all around her. It was like the mist that hung over the ocean, and she imagined that she could even scoop it up and put it in her pockets to take home and save. It had a smell of incense, candles, and peace.

She took off her squishing shoes and noiselessly glided through the fragrant silence into one of the pews in the back. She wasn't sure exactly how to pray, but she squeezed her eyes shut and thought hard about Eddie. She wished with all her might that he was well. She was probably doing it all wrong. It felt too much like throwing a penny in the fountain at the mall and wishing for a friend, or crossing all her fingers in hopes that her father wouldn't be in an angry mood. She had done those things when she was younger, when she believed in magic and fairy tale rescues. Praying needed something different, and she had never learned it.

Maybe it was too late for her. Maybe God didn't listen, turned away from someone like her, someone with a blackness growing inside. She flexed her right hand. It was already sore from hitting Frankie's face. Frankie had been mean, cruel to her even, over the last two years. But he had never once hit her. She was worse than Frankie Marzano. But the thing that scared her the most was that a part of her was glad she had hit him and thirsted to do it again.

Carly dropped onto the cushioned kneeler. It felt holier to kneel. "I'm sorry, I'm sorry, I'm sorry," she whispered. "Just please let Eddie be okay, and I'll never do it again. Amen."

Time was running out. She slipped out of the pew and walked softly to the front of the church. She pulled Eddie's wallet out of her pocket and set it on the altar. The priest would find it and give it to Eddie or to the police. It was the best she could do. She put her water-logged shoes back on her feet. She opened the side door and was blasted once more by the rain and the wind. She had to get home. The storm was definitely getting worse.

With the water rising almost to her knees in some low-lying streets, it seemed like forever before she made it to the candy shop. The little bell on the door tinkled, announcing her arrival.

Her father appeared in the office doorway, his unshaven face black with whiskers. "It's about time."

She threw the door shut. "Yeah, well, it's hard getting around out there, you know." Carly felt her voice rising and paused to regain some control. "Some of the streets are totally flooded. I had to go blocks out of my way."

"Yeah. I figured as much," he said. "Wait there a minute." He disappeared into his office and came back out with an old towel. "Dry off there by the door. I don't want you dripping all over the house." He tossed the towel to her. "Then go up and start packing up your stuff."

"Packing?"

"Yes. Packing. As soon as this storm clears out, we're going."

Carly's heart dropped. She draped the towel over her head to hide the pain she knew must be showing on her face. She put her hand in her pocket, feeling around for the comforting silence from the church, but it had all leaked away. She should have taken a prayer book and a handful of sand, a conch shell and a jar of ocean water. She wanted to hold on to it all, to every little piece. The shelves beside her had already been cleared. All that was left were the thin dust lines that marked the boundaries between boxes of saltwater taffy. She dragged the towel behind her and slowly climbed the back steps.

"Mom?" Carly knocked softly on her mother's bedroom door. There was no answer. "Mom?" Cocking her head toward the stairs and hearing nothing of her father, she gently opened the door and tiptoed over to the bed. Her mother was lying still, eyes closed, her face white and pale in the darkness and her mouth half open. Small beads of perspiration dotted her forehead, and damp strands of dark hair clung to her cheeks. Her mother never slept during the day. She never even sat down when there was work to be done. Her clothes still hung in the closet, shoes lined neatly on the floor. Her creams and powders and bottles sat unpacked on the bureau. Something was wrong. But she couldn't bring herself to wake her mother. She would wait and watch.

Carly slowly climbed the next flight of steps to her attic room, but she didn't pack. It wouldn't take her long anyway. Other than her books, she had nothing but a few drawers of old clothes. No trinkets or toys, no make-up or nail polish, no posters to remove carefully from the walls. The things she cared about most were already packed away in her memory, the sounds and smell of the ocean, the feel of the mist, the long, white glow of the moon on the water. She would never forget the feeling of Nick's hand in her own or the roll of Eddie's laugh. Poor Eddie. She was desperate to know how he was, to go away with a memory of him happily selling papers from his stand.

Carly changed out of her wet clothes and hung them out on the stair banister to dry. Her room was already filled with an overpowering musty smell that the wet clothes would only make worse.

She paced the floor, pulling a brush through her hair over and over until her scalp tingled. She heard her father moving about the house, clearing out closets and drawers. She heard the pull and rip of the packing tape, a sound as familiar to her as lullabies and nursery rhymes were to other children. She stood at the window and looked down at the tree through the smear of rain. The wind lashed at the helpless branches and they rocked back and forth on the ground. Poor tree.

"Carly!"

Carly dropped the brush and ran to her door.

Her mother stood at the bottom of the stairs. "How about some lunch?"

Carly jumped down the steps.

"I'm so glad you're back!" Mrs. Chambers' face was

pale, her eyes puffy. She squeezed Carly's arm. "I was so worried about you out there."

"But you were asleep." Carly looked down at the floor. "I thought you were hurt or something."

"I was never asleep. I was just resting my eyes. Come on in the kitchen." Mrs. Chambers slid her hand in the refrigerator and quickly pulled out some lunch meat and sodas. "How about a turkey sandwich? The drinks are still cold. I'm afraid if the electricity stays out much longer, though, the food's going to spoil."

Mrs. Chambers suddenly seemed to lose her balance and grabbed the counter.

"Are you okay?" Carly took the bread bag from her mother's hands. "You should sit down. I'll make the sandwiches."

Mrs. Chambers didn't protest and slid into a kitchen chair. "Just make one for yourself. I'm not too hungry."

"Are you sure you're not hurt?" Carly sat across the table from her. "Is it because of Dad..." She lowered her voice, ". . .hitting you?"

"He didn't!" Mrs. Chambers hissed. "It was because I lost my balance. And the floor was wet! I told you. Besides, it has nothing to do with my head. It's...it's something else. It will pass. In a little while, it will pass." She pushed the damp strands of hair back from her eyes. "Maybe I should have some crackers."

Carly felt around in the dark cabinet for the box of saltines and brought them to her mother. Her mother ate a few, pausing to sit with her head in her hands.

Then she abruptly jumped up from the table and left the room.

"Where's your mother?" Mr. Chambers wandered into the kitchen, packing tape in one hand, a file box under his arm.

"Bedroom." Carly jerked her thumb to the left. "Is there something..." Her words trailed off to silence. Her father had turned his back and headed off down the hall toward the bedroom.

Carly sat alone at the kitchen table. The storm outside noisily battered the walls and rattled the old windows, while the silence inside only grew and grew. Her fingers closed around the loaf of bread, sinking into the slices, squeezing until there was nothing left but a lumpy mess. How can you just pretend that nothing is happening, Nick had said. Carly thought of the money in the box. Was that what her father did in the cellar, made money? Carly stood. She hid the misshapen bread bag in the bottom of the trashcan and went up to her bedroom. She couldn't pretend anymore. She *was* curious. She wanted to know about the money and about what went on in the cellar. She would wait for the night. She was used to the dark. She had grown up in it.

# CHAPTER 24

Carly cracked her bedroom door open and stood silently, listening. Her clock was frozen at twenty past three from last night when the light died and the tree had split. She had no watch, but she felt that it was late, very late. Still, she waited, straining for any sound. Without electricity, there was no television, no click of a keyboard to pinpoint her father's location. What if he were sitting on the couch in the darkness, brooding or making plans?

Carly inched the door open wider and slipped out into the hall. She leaned against the wall, wiping her damp palms across her shorts. Maybe this was all a mistake. She should just go back into her room and shut the door and forget about it. They would be moving soon anyway. She could leave all her questions behind, locked in this old house. But she couldn't. She had to know, even if the knowledge turned out to be bitter.

She pushed herself away from the wall and started down the stairs. Her feet were bare. It was easier to be silent that way, feeling carefully around the creaking boards and over any clutter that might have been left in unforeseen places. Like a cat, she knew where to place each foot. She avoided the loose board on the fifth step and the raised nail on the eighth. At the bottom of the steps she stood quietly, peering down the dark hall at her parents' closed bedroom door. She heard her father's low, rhythmic snoring. She quickly glided through the back hall and down into the shop.

A sudden rattle startled her, but it was only a gust of wind against the shop door. The cellar was always locked and her father normally opened it with one of the keys on the chain he kept in his pants' pocket. But she knew there was a spare. A two-drawer file cabinet was wedged in a corner behind the counter. A coffee pot sat on top of it. Sometimes he pretended that he had dropped a cup or a coin before reaching his hand in the back and coming up with the key concealed in his palm. She wasn't quite as stupid as he thought.

Carly held her breath and dropped her arm down the back of the cabinet, careful to avoid brushing the pot and the assortment of cups that littered its top. She felt nothing but the cool, smooth metal. She leaned farther, her hand almost reaching the floor before she felt it. It was attached to a small magnet and had slid close to the bottom. She squeezed it in her damp fist and tiptoed to the cellar door. She eased the key into the lock and turned it gently until she heard a click. The door slowly creaked open. She paused, holding her breath. Did he hear? But the house remained silent.

Carly took the flashlight from the counter and pointed the yellow beam down into the cellar. She would have to be careful on these steps. She had never been on them before and didn't know the pattern of creaks. She hugged the rail, putting most of her weight on it, and lightly descended on the edge of each step. There was an earthy smell down here, like potting soil stacked in the garden shed. The floor was concrete and felt cool on the bottoms of her feet.

She shone the flashlight around. The cellar was small. The walls looked like nothing more than packed dirt. The low ceiling was wooden and wires trailed across the beams and hung down here and there like snakes. Two long folding tables and two white plastic chairs sat in the middle of the room. In the corner, boxes were piled four or five deep. Carly focused the light on each box in turn. They were all plain and unmarked, all sealed tightly with packing tape. She was too late. He had already packed everything up. If she opened a box, he would know. She risked coming down here for nothing.

Suddenly, there was a loud swoosh of water over her head. She jumped and dropped the flashlight on her foot and it went out. A small cry escaped her lips. It was only the pipes. But that meant that someone in the house had just flushed the toilet or used a sink. Someone was awake and moving around. Carly felt around in the darkness for the flashlight and limped to the stairs. She took the steps two at a time, heedless of the creaking, shut and locked the door, and replaced the key behind the file cabinet. She could come up with lots of excuses for being in the shop in the middle of the night, but none for being in the cellar.

She went noiselessly up the stairs to the kitchen. She stood just around the corner from the hall and listened. There were voices in her parents' bedroom. Had they heard anything? She crept across the hall and toward the stairs to her bedroom. A light appeared under her parents' door and heavy footsteps tramped around the room. Carly dashed up the steps. She accidentally hit something at the top, and she heard a faint clinking noise as it fell, hitting the wooden steps. A door opened below. There was no time to retrieve whatever it was. She slipped into her room and silently slid the lock into place. She flopped on her bed and stared at the ceiling, the flashlight still gripped in her right hand.

# CHAPTER 25

Carly must have drifted off to sleep, because she jumped up, confused, wondering where she was, when the pounding began on her bedroom door.

"Open this door! Now!" Her father was shouting.

Carly clutched her pillow to her chest. The flashlight was still clasped in her right hand. She couldn't seem to relax her grip on it.

"You have five seconds," he screamed, "or I'll break down this goddamn door."

She stood motionless beside her bed, unable to speak, her mouth half open. She must have disturbed something in the cellar. He must have discovered it. And it was all for nothing. She didn't even see anything down there. In a few seconds, her door began to tremble and splinter. It was very old. A good kick would surely dislodge the lock.

Carly went for the window. She pulled the wet towel from the opening, but the door sprung open before she could climb out. He stood there in the entrance, panting like a wounded tiger. Without thinking what she was doing, Carly flung the flashlight at him with all her might and hit him square in the head. He stumbled back and fell to the floor with a thud. She stood paralyzed, gazing at her hand, still bruised from hitting Frankie, as though it were some foreign object that had suddenly grown from the end of her arm. Her father groaned and raised himself on one elbow. She had a fantastic urge to kick him back down again, out into the hall and down the stairs. The feeling swirled in her, like a hurricane, wild and heedless, but in the center, she felt herself icy cold. Like father, like daughter.

Her father sat up and shook his head. Looking at him she began to see herself, old and thick, the dark angers of her life lining her face in a permanent ugly scowl, frightening even those few people who wanted to love her, perhaps her own innocent children. His body was blocking the door. She squeezed out the window and moved carefully across the roof. The rain had finally stopped, but the wind came in occasional gusts, blowing her hair back from her face. There was nowhere for her to go, no tree to climb down, no escape. She gazed across the yard to Aileen's house, but there was no candlelight behind the windows. It didn't matter anyway. She couldn't hide in Aileen's room or anywhere else. She would have to face him somehow when he came out, and she knew that he would.

She heard him struggling to open the swollen window, banging and cursing. Finally, his head appeared out the window and he called her names she had never even heard before.

"Don't come out!" Carly yelled. "Leave me alone!"

But she watched him push against the window frame, squeezing one shoulder through and then the next. Carly looked over the side. It was a long way down. She moved all the way to the far edge of the roof.

"So, what did you tell him?" he snarled, pulling his last leg through the window.

"Tell who?" Carly asked, confused.

"Don't play games with me," he snapped, gripping the window frame for balance. "I'll get it out of you one way or another."

"I don't know what you're talking about!" Carly pulled her knees to her chest and held them tightly.

Her father put his hand in his shirt pocket. He drew out a card, and held it toward her. It was too dark to see, but she knew instantly what it was—the tall man's card. She had completely forgotten. She left them in the pocket of the wet pants that she had hung over the rail to dry. That must have been what fell when she snuck back into her room. She had knocked the pants down the stairs, dislodging the cards from her pocket. Or maybe he saw the shorts on the floor and searched the pockets. This wasn't about the cellar at all. This was worse. Even the truth wouldn't help her—that she had told nothing, protected her father and all their family secrets, carrying them like weights hung around her neck. He would never believe her.

Her father crumbled the card in his fist and stuffed it back into his pocket. "What did they promise you, a few candy bars? A night on the boardwalk?" He turned his head and spit over the side of the roof. "You're a traitor to your own family."

"I didn't tell him anything." Carly began to cry, hard, deep sobs that she couldn't control. "But I wish I had," she choked. "I wish they had come and taken you away!" She looked up at him sharply. "I know what was in that box. I know what you do."

Her father stood silently. It was too dark to see his face, but she was sure it was mottled with the red splotches that always betrayed his anger. He turned his head and looked around the roof and shifted his feet. Finally, he reached out his hand to her. "It's okay, Carly. I'm not mad anymore. Just come back inside, and we'll talk about it." He tried to keep his voice even, but she wasn't fooled. "Come on," he urged. "I'm worried about you out here."

"No, you're not," Carly shot back, sniffling. "You're worried about you out here." She saw how stiffly he stood, how rigidly he gripped the window frame. "I'm not coming back in," she insisted. "Not ever."

"We'll see about that," he exploded, slamming his fist against the side of the house.

He slowly released the window frame and took a few baby steps toward her, his fingers gripping at the wall. He was headed straight for the loose tiles. He would never see them in the dark. Carly's eyes widened, but she held her lips tightly closed. He would surely fall. It would serve him right too. He deserved it. It wouldn't be her fault. It wouldn't be like she actually pushed him. She did warn him. She told him not to come out.

But she felt a tightness spreading, weblike, across her face and a black pool of bitterness settling in the pit of her stomach. She jumped up.

"Stop!" she shouted, grabbing the side of the house. "The tiles are loose there, right in front of you. You'll slip."

Her father smiled. She saw the white of his teeth in the darkness. "You think I'm an idiot? I'm not that easily fooled."

"But I'm not kidding!" Carly insisted. "It's really true. I've been out here plenty of times before."

They stood facing each other, about twelve feet apart. It was still dark, but the dawn was coming. A faint glow was rising behind her on the ocean. She saw it reflected in his eyes.

"Don't do it," Carly begged. He gave a small laugh and took another step toward her. The tile immediately slid out from beneath him, and he let out a sharp cry. His arms flailed helplessly in the air, but there was nothing to hold and his heavy body tumbled to the edge of the roof. He was dangling, his fingers cupped inside the aluminum rain gutter that ran the length of the roof.

"Carly! Carly, do something!" he screamed.

She scrambled carefully across the roof and stared down at him.

"Carly!" He was strong. His legs were frantically kicking, trying to get a foothold somehow against the side of the house. But the eaves were too wide and he couldn't make it.

Carly dropped flat on the roof and flung her arms

over the side, gripping his arms the best she could.

"Pull!" he yelled. "If I can just get my elbows up over the edge." He was panting and swinging his legs like a child hanging from the monkey bars.

"Harder! Harder!" he demanded.

She couldn't stand up. She knew she'd be pitched right over the side. But pulling while lying on her stomach was not very effective.

There was a sudden screech and a low groan as the rain gutter he was clutching began to pull away from the house. "Hold on! Hold on to me!" he called frantically.

But there was nothing she could do. He was slipping. He grabbed her right arm and she felt herself being pulled down with him. If she didn't let go, they would fall together. Her head and shoulders were already off the roof. "I can't!" she screamed. "I can't! Let go of me!"

He clutched at her, his nails digging deeply into her arm. She wrenched herself free. The gutter gave way and her father fell, with a loud crack, into the remains of the downed tree.

# CHAPTER 26

The yellow of the rising sun mingled with the blue and red of the flashing lights, and everything swam. Carly felt as though she were watching it all from the bottom of a deep pool of water. Faces dipped in and out. Voices floated past. Clangs, sirens, and shouts splashed somewhere far above.

It was the shrill, insistent screaming that made her turn her head and try to focus. She was stretched out on the front lawn, an IV line trailing up her arm and into the hands of the man who crouched beside her. A nail from the loosened gutter had caught her as it pulled away from the house, ripping a gash from elbow to wrist. That much she remembered. The hot pain was there, and she wanted to drift back into the bottom of the pool where everything was blurred. But the screaming kept her up.

There was a crowd of people milling about, staring at her, held back by police.

"But she's my sister! I'm telling you, she's my sister and I need to talk to her!" the voice shrieked.

Carly followed it and saw Aileen, arms flailing, hair bouncing, at the front of the crowd. She darted toward Carly.

"Hey!" yelled the man with the IV.

"Here. Hold this." Aileen pulled a gob of gum from her mouth and held it out toward the man, dropping it in the grass beside him when he lurched away from it.

"They took him first! Can you believe it? They gave him the first ambulance." Aileen looked up at the man with the IV bag. "What the hell's the matter with you people?"

"Can someone get her out of here?" called the man.

Aileen leaned down and whispered to Carly. "I heard him when they were taking him away. He said he was up on the roof trying to *help* you. He said that you have a problem with…"

A police officer dropped his hand on Aileen's shoulder and ordered her up. "C'mon now," he said. "You're not her sister. Get back. That's enough."

Aileen locked her eyes on Carly's. "We are sisters. You know we are."

Aileen disappeared and Carly closed her eyes, dropping back down to the bottom of the pool, deeper and deeper until everything was gone.

# CHAPTER 27

Carly jolted awake, then lay still for a moment in the darkness, getting her bearings and listening to the bustle and low voices coming from the nurses' station down the hall. The IV pole was beside her bed, the bag half full, dripping clear liquid through a tube into the back of her hand. She wasn't sure what it was for, but she'd have to live without it. She picked at the corner of the tape, then carefully ripped it off. She could see the needle threaded into her vein and turned away, suddenly nauseous. She clenched her jaw and jerked the needle out, a hot pain like the flash of a match burning into her skin. Blood squirted out where the needle had been, and she quickly pressed it with the edge of her sheet. She counted to ten and prayed it would stop. It did. This was her chance.

She had faded in and out of sleep for the past two days, eavesdropping on all the quiet conversations that went on in her room. She was very good at feigning sleep—long, slow, even breaths, half-open mouth and perfectly still eyelids. She ignored the doctors and nurses, her mother, and, most especially, the detectives and social workers who wanted to ask her a few questions, to counsel her. She couldn't talk to anyone until she had time to figure things out, and she had been too groggy. What could she say? Why had she been on the roof? How did he fall? How did she get hurt? She needed time to build up the wall of stories and explanations, to make it firm and hide herself and the embarrassing truths behind it.

One thing she had learned from her eavesdropping was that her father was here too, one floor up, Room 538. Her mother had spent the last two days shuttling between rooms. But Carly would have known he was in the hospital even without overhearing, and felt his presence even if there were fifty floors of concrete between them. The thought of him weighed heavily on her and was one of the things that made it so easy to feign sleep.

She slipped out of bed and quietly opened the drawer that held the things her mother had brought: toothbrush, comb, clean clothes. She was lightheaded and steadied herself against the chest. It would feel good to get out of the stupid hospital gown. She didn't know why they called it a gown. It was more like a large napkin with a few snaps sewn onto it. Even Aileen would be embarrassed by its skimpiness.

Getting to the elevator would be the hard part. Once she was in the lobby though, she knew she'd make it. She had to get out. She needed fresh air and quiet. It was impossible to think in the hospital with people constantly hovering over her bed.

She slipped to the edge of the door and watched the hall. Maybe she'd never come back at all. She had a grandmother in Florida. She knew the address from the yearly Christmas cards and vaguely remembered the face from when she was a small child. It was a long shot, but it might be worth a try. She had nothing to lose. Nothing at all. Nick would lend her the money she needed to get there and keep quiet about it. She hoped.

The nurses were at the station. She stood watching them, waiting for the right time. One woman pulled a picture out of her purse, and they all bent low, oohing and aahing over it. It was now or never. Carly slid out the door and down the hall, quickly and quietly, patient rooms swimming past her. She rounded a corner and faced the elevators. She jabbed at the button, head down, until the *ding* rang out. The sound bounced off the ceiling and walls, like an alarm announcing her escape. The doors swooshed open. She jumped in and pressed herself against the side of the elevator, praying that no one was coming. It felt like an hour, but the doors finally slid shut and the elevator sat, humming, at her command. Her finger hovered over "L" for Lobby, but for some reason she couldn't push it. She was breathing hard. Her hand trailed up to "5," fifth floor, and hung for a few moments in the air. Then she hit 5 hard with the heel of her hand and jumped back as the elevator lurched upward, and her stomach did too.

Just outside the elevator there was a cart piled with clean sheets and towels. She pulled several off the top of the stack and tried to look official as she carried them down the hall, searching for 538. Her disguise was lousy and totally unnecessary. The second room she came to was 538. But she hesitated outside the door, biting her thumbnail. She had just turned to leave when she heard the *ding* of the elevator. Someone would be rounding the corner any second. She had no choice. She glanced up the hall toward the nurses' station, then slipped into her father's room.

He didn't see her at first. The room was dark except for the glow from the small television that hung from the ceiling, its volume on low. He looked odd, like a cartoon man squeezed into a toy bed, his bulky frame tucked under the thin, faded hospital blankets, big feet poking up at the end. An IV dripped into his arm. What was she doing here? She squeezed the towels to her chest, her palms damp with sweat, and decided to back out the door.

But he turned his head. She saw a quick flash in his eyes, or perhaps it was just the light reflected from the television, and then a broad smile spread across his face.

"Carly! Pumpkin! How'd you get here? How are you feeling?"

Pumpkin. He hadn't called her that since she was four or five. Tiny voices from the TV speaker squeaked in the background, but she couldn't find her own voice. She just stood and stared.

There were two days worth of whiskers on his chin, casting the whole bottom half of his face in shadow. "Honey, pull that chair up next to my bed and have a seat.

I've been so worried about you."

Worried about me? That sounded familiar. Carly's head felt light, dizzy.

"C'mon, pull the chair over," he insisted. "Sit down."

She turned, still gripping her towels, and squeaked the small wooden chair from the corner, stopping just short of the bed. She sat stiffly, on the edge of the seat.

"So, tell me how you're feeling," he asked.

His eyes moved, and sometimes his head. But the rest was very still. She gazed at his legs, hidden under the blankets.

"Well? Tell me."

Carly cleared her throat. "Okay, I guess. It's just my arm." She fingered the bandage that ran from wrist to elbow. "I think a nail from the rain gutter got it." She heard again that slow, screeching groan, the ancient gutter pulling away from the house, and felt her stomach flip, like a pancake. She shot him a quick glance, but his face was still, his eyes too hard to read.

"And you...?" she began.

"Ah, don't worry about me. Messed up my legs and a disk in my back, but I'll be fixed up and running fine in no time. Guaranteed." He sounded like a used car commercial.

"Your mom says that the doctors were worried you might have an infection in that arm. Here, let me see." He reached his hand out toward her, but she sat motionless, out of reach.

"I said, let me see."

"No." It came out too loud, too short. "It's fine."

His hand hung for a moment in the empty air between them, then he slowly drew it back to his side. "I think they must have bombarded you with drugs to kill the infection. That's probably why. That explains it." He turned his head from her and stared up at the ceiling.

She knew her line. She was supposed to say "Explains what?" But she never did like her part in that play. She wasn't quite sure what had made her come to his room, but she knew now that it was a mistake. She stood up, changed the script, jumped to the final act. "I better go."

"Carly!" He turned to her, forced to improvise. "Don't go. Listen, honey. Things are going to be better for us. I mean it. As soon as I get out of here, we'll go on a nice vacation. Would you like that? Someplace fun. Maybe we'll go out west." His words were coming fast, his right arm gripping the bed rail.

She stood still, running her hand through the towels, halfway between the bed and the door.

"Carly? What do you think?" The car commercial voice was gone. He was smoother now, selling insurance, peace of mind, a vision of a secure future. Limited time offer. Don't pass it up.

She dropped her eyes to the floor. Could they really be a happy family, driving off on a vacation, the suitcases in the trunk, singing along with the radio? She looked up at him, searched his face. It was what she always wanted. "I like the beach," she offered.

"Okay! Good. We'll go to a beach. But listen." He dropped his voice to a whisper. "I need you to do me a favor first. An *important* favor. People are going to ask you questions. Did you know that?"

She knew.

"You don't tell them anything in particular about your deliveries or the boxes, okay? I'll take care of it. You just say you delivered candy all over Oceanside and that's that. That's all you know. You don't remember anything else."

"And the money...?"

"Just forget about that. It's nothing. Pretend you never saw it. You're just a kid. It's a complicated business thing that you don't understand. I'll take care of it all."

Carly's head was heavy. She dropped her face into the towels, taking deep breaths of the fresh laundry smell, wishing it were ether, sucking out her memory. She could start all over again, a happy family on a car ride, headed west. No past, no pain, no anger.

"And the roof. Carly, look at me."

But she kept her face in the towels, squeezing them tight to her eyes, working hard on the impossible dream.

"I told the police that we were checking the loose tiles after the storm, checking for water damage. You were helping me, right? Do you remember that?"

She shook her head, towels and all.

"Yes, you do! You have to remember that. We were worried about leaks."

Carly groaned. Leaks of family secrets, maybe. At least it was partly true.

"You listen to me," he sputtered. "I did you a favor. I could have told them that you pushed me and gotten you sent away for a while. I could have. You're a troubled child, Carly. They'd have believed me."

Carly slowly let the towel slip from her face and raised her head to look at him.

"It's true and you know it. But I didn't do it. I'm counting on you now." The lights from the television flickered on his face, light then dark, his eyes turning from red to green to black. "Can you hand me that tissue box there?"

He did her a favor? He could have hurt her bad, made up a vicious story of what happened on the roof, and gotten her in trouble. He was right. It probably would have worked. Who would ever believe her? He passed up a good opportunity to hurt her, and so she owed him some lies in return. She was having trouble with his logic.

"Come on. Please? I need a tissue." He sniffled a few times. "The least you can do is hand me a tissue."

She shuffled to the tray table and retrieved the small box, holding it out to him at arm's length. But he ignored the tissues and made a grab for her wrist instead, yanking her to his side. His mouth had disappeared beneath the whiskers, his lips pressed into a thin, tight line, and beads of perspiration dotted his forehead.

"I need you to do what I say, Carly." He shook her arm. "Now repeat for me what you're going to say."

She tugged at her arm, but he wouldn't let go. Even on his back in a hospital bed he was stronger.

"You owe me, Carly. You owe me big time."

In the dim light, she saw the muscles in his face twitching.

"I took care of you all these years. Fed you. Clothed you. You'd be in the gutter if it wasn't for me. You and your mother both. And what did you ever give me in return but those surly looks?"

Carly's mouth went dry, her blood cold.

"You owe me. Do you hear?" He was breathing hard and fast, like a bull in the ring. "Okay?" He shook her again. "Okay?"

She nodded, not sure what she was agreeing to. He loosened his hold and she pulled free, dropping the towels. She backed away from him and stumbled out of the room into the hall.

"Carly! Carly!" he shouted. "Wait!"

Carly took off down the hall, squinting in the glare of the florescent lights. She skipped the elevator and went for the stairs, running down flight after flight, around and around, everything spinning. She came out the back exit of the hospital. She weaved through the cars in the parking lot like a mouse in a maze and found herself on the lawns of a large park. She ignored the paths and made straight for the lake, taking comfort in the darkness that enveloped her like an old friend.

She walked along the edge of the water until the bank became overgrown and the lake met the woods. She pushed up past the shrubbery and wandered aimlessly through the trees. Exhausted and numb, she came to a clearing of tall grasses and sank down into it. She lay back and stared up at the sky. She had to figure out what to do, where to go. But her head was too heavy and the darkness was swallowing her up.

# CHAPTER 28

Carly woke with a start. She was stiff and sore from sleeping on the ground and the sun was blazing down on her face. Something buzzed in her ear. She stretched and then stood, the gnats rising with her.

She hiked back down through the trees to the lake and walked around the edge of the water to the park. She needed to get out to the highway and follow it to Oceanside. If she could find Nick, he might hide her for a few days until she could figure out what to do. As she came out of the woods, she noticed someone standing just off the path ahead of her, next to a bench, throwing stones into the lake. He turned to stare at her and she flinched. What was he doing here?

The first stone hit her in the chest. The second one narrowly missed her eye.

"Knock it off," she yelled, covering her face.

"Why should I?" Frankie asked menacingly, raising a clenched fist toward her.

Carly peeked at him from between her fingers and noticed the cut under his left eye, the raised red lump from where she had hit him. She remembered and shrunk back. They almost matched, his-and-her bruises.

He turned from her and started throwing the rocks out into the lake. His baggy shorts were rumpled and dirty and it looked like he hadn't changed his T-shirt in days. Maybe he had slept in the woods too. She should have just turned her back on him and walked quickly away. But something held her there. He wasn't just Frankie anymore. He was the kid whose picture was in Eddie's wallet.

Frankie reached down to the ground for more rocks. "They're looking for you, you know," he said without looking up.

Carly glanced over her shoulder. The park was empty. "Who? What are you talking about?"

"Everybody. Nurses. Doctors. Police. It's like a zoo in there." Frankie nodded his head in the direction of the hospital.

Carly's eyes grew wide.

"I hear they're gonna put up Wanted posters too." Frankie began talking in a high nasal voice. "Girl missing from hospital. Extremely ugly. Infected with a terminal case of nerdiness. Anyone with information please call the police—or the dog pound."

Frankie threw his head back and let out several howls, like a wolf. "You're lucky there's no reward involved or I'd be dragging you in there myself."

Carly licked her lips. "Frankie, you're lying, right? It's not funny, you know."

He turned and glared at her, jiggling the stones in

218

his hand. For a minute she thought that he was going to fling the whole bunch at her. "Listen, Chambers, I don't care whether you believe me or not. For all I care you could go drown yourself in this lake."

Carly began to pace around the bench. "But why? Why should they care where I am? It's not like I'm seriously injured or anything."

Frankie's eyebrows were up and he was staring hard at her. "I don't know. The whole thing seems pretty suspicious to me. It's the only reason I'm not smashing your face into the ground right now. Then they'd blame me for being involved in the other stuff, whatever it is." He put his foot up on the bench and leaned in toward her. "So what'd you do, Chambers?"

Carly gripped the back of the bench and returned his stare. "I didn't do anything."

"Yeah, right. It's a pretty good line. But when they catch you, I'd try to come up with something a little more creative than that." Frankie stalked over to a mesh trash container, grabbed the top, and began dragging it toward the lake. Carly watched him struggle with the trashcan at the shore, trying to raise it over his head. What was he doing here? This park was on the mainland, over the causeway, at least twenty minutes from where they lived. She doubted he traveled that far just for vandalism and he sure didn't come out to visit her.

With a grunt, Frankie tried to throw the can out into the lake. It splashed in just at the edge, the soda cans, napkins, newspapers, and juice boxes floating out from it like an oil slick from a grounded tanker. They both stood there, watching the spreading trash, the water lapping at and rocking the whole mess.

"So what are you doing here?" Carly asked.

Frankie jammed his hands in his pockets and stared at her with his small gray eyes. "Same thing as you are," he finally answered. "Out here is better than in there." He jerked his head in the direction of the hospital.

"You can say that again," Carly sighed.

Frankie pointed out across the park. "See the tops of those buildings over there?"

"Yeah?"

"It's the Tri-County Mall. Bus runs back to Oceanside every hour or so. You can catch it in front of the Eckard's Drug Store."

Carly stared at him, open-mouthed.

Frankie shrugged. "In case you wanted to slip out of here."

Her heart jumped. "But I don't have any money."

Frankie smirked, but he dug his hands into his pockets and pulled out several crumpled up dollar bills, holding them out toward her.

Carly hesitated, waiting for the punch line, but nothing came. She took the money from him before he changed his mind. "Why are you doing this?" she asked. "Why would you want to help me?"

"Don't get any stupid ideas, Chambers," he said. "I hate your guts. But I ain't no big fan of the Oceanside police either. I don't know what you did, but I hope it was real good."

He thought she did something criminal, and maybe

he was right. She didn't really know. Carly put the money in her pocket and started toward the mall. She stopped and turned back toward Frankie. "How come you're hanging out at the hospital?" She looked him up and down. "Are you sick or something?"

Frankie snorted and stared out across the lake. "My mom's in there visiting with your buddy, the fat man. They know each other from their past or something. She made me come, but there's no way I'm hanging out in his room with nothing to do but look at his fat face."

Of course Eddie would be there! Beach Memorial was the only hospital for miles around. Carly laced her fingers together, squeezing. "How is he? Is he okay?"

"What do I look like, the president of his fan club? I hate the guy, okay?" Frankie picked up a bottle that had floated toward the water's edge and smashed it against a rock. "I don't care how he's doing. He must've told my mom some stuff about me throwing magazines around, 'cause now she's going to make me work at his stupid newspaper stand."

Frankie began to attack the bench, kicking at the wooden slats, splintering the arm rests.

Carly shook her head. "He's a really good guy, you know."

"Maybe to a nerd like you he is," Frankie spat back at her. His face was covered with sweat, and he attacked the bench with renewed violence.

"If you'd just give him half a chance, you'd like him," she shouted. "And he's... he's..." She had to clamp her mouth shut, hard. And he's your father! She could see it so clearly now. The resemblance was there, from the slump of his shoulders to the shape of his thick eyebrows.

Frankie whipped around toward her. "Just SHUT UP!" he screamed.

He stood there trembling with anger or fear, like a deer on the highway, lost in the headlights. And all these years Eddie just watched from a distance. How could he? What gave parents the right to keep those kinds of secrets? It wasn't fair.

She was going to give him the truth, even if he punched her in the face for it. "Listen, Frankie. I got something to tell you."

"NO!" He stepped toward her, both hands curled into fists. "*You* listen, Chambers. I'm sick of looking at your ugly face. I'm sick of hearing your stupid voice. You got that?" He gave her a hard shove in the chest and she stumbled backward, almost falling. "So get *lost!*" He dropped onto the bench and carefully fingered the damaged armrest, plucking splinters like a surgeon.

Carly steadied herself and opened her mouth, but he shot her a menacing look, his eyes two dark slits, his forehead tight waves of clenched skin. Then he turned away and rested his chin in his hands. His fingers crawled up over his ears, closing her out.

She watched him for a moment, bent over and slack, his large T-shirt hanging damply from his frame. He seemed almost to be melting, an icicle in August, all cold and angry hot, coming loose. She left him and walked off through the trees, cradling her sore arm. She pushed on through the park, avoiding the paths, stumbling through the undergrowth. She couldn't remember the last time she'd eaten. Her legs were shaky and her head swam. Despite the heat, a cold sweat broke out on her forehead and down the back of her neck. Waves of nausea rolled around her empty stomach. She had to rest a little before going on. She collapsed on the ground amongst some bushes, hidden, halfway between the mall and the hospital, breathing hard.

She hung her head between her knees and plucked at the grass. She trailed her fingers through the weeds and dirt, disturbing a column of black ants. They ran past her feet and then back again, up over the mountain of her shoe, down and up and over and over. Why did they do that, run pell-mell, zigzag in the same small spot like windup toys gone crazy? Maybe they were lost. How could you ever find your way in a forest of grass?

She thought of Frankie telling her to get lost. But the joke was on him. She was already lost, entangled in the thorny secrets and lies that surrounded her life. Back and forth, in and out, around and around, just like these ants. She had no idea where she was, where she was going. She didn't even know who she was anymore.

She fell back in the grass and stared up at the sky, blue and cloudless. In the distance she heard the traffic humming on Route 72, cars and buses heading to and from the island. She reached in her pocket and felt the crumpled dollar bills. She pulled them out and smoothed them between her hands. Were they real or fake? How could anyone tell? They looked just the same. She held up her own five-fingered hands, her pale-skinned, freckled, once broken, always empty arms. Was she real or only counterfeit? Her life was built on a mountain of lies and excuses. Was she a troubled child or the child of a troubled man? How could she tell? It was like wandering in the house of mirrors. It all depended on your angle and line of sight. But something had to be real. Didn't it?

Carly slowly pushed herself off the ground and stood shakily in the hush of the park, hugging her arms to her body. The heat hung on her like an iron blanket and the sun sat on her head like a too-tight hat. The air was heavy and still, as though this whole day just stopped for a moment and held its breath, waiting. And she knew. The dollar bills all damp and creased in her hand were real—crumpled and worn—but still real and valuable. Unlike her stiff and freshly minted lies, they held up, lasted, and didn't crumble to nothing. Because they were real.

Panic attacked her insides like a swarm of moths, but she turned away from the mall, the bus, the hiding and the running, the secrets and lies, and walked in a straight line toward the hospital. She hadn't prepared any stories or elaborate excuses. She was going to tell the truth, simple and plain, no matter what she was asked, no matter what it cost. Her legs nearly folded under her as she approached the building, her eyes focused on the fifth floor, but she bit hard on her lower lip and forced herself forward. Brick walls were crumbling inside her, silence falling down.

# CHAPTER 29

It was a family reunion. After the doctors checked Carly over, a nurse wheeled her to room 538. The lights were bright, the television off.

"I don't need the wheelchair," Carly insisted. "I can stand on my own."

"Okay, honey," the nurse replied. "But you be careful. She turned to Carly's parents. "Doctor says she's just fine, nothing to worry about. But we're going to keep her a little while for observation."

The nurse rested her hand on Carly's shoulder. "I'll be back for you in ten minutes or so. Mom and Dad will take care of you till then."

Mr. Chambers smiled up at them from his bed. "Don't worry. We'll take real good care of her."

Mrs. Chambers was shaking. She finally collapsed in heavy sobs, holding Carly tightly. The nurse left, closing the door behind her with a soft click.

"That's enough, Leila," Mr. Chambers barked. "I told you she was fine. She was just putting on a little show for the sympathy."

Carly felt her mother's arms loosen, then drop away from her. Mrs. Chambers grabbed her purse, rooting through it for a handkerchief, then settled into a chair in the corner, sniffing and drying her eyes.

Carly stood alone in the middle of the room.

Her father stared at her, propped up in his bed like a king, pillows behind his head and back. He crossed his arms on his chest. "So, you had your fun," he said. "Look at your mother. Go ahead. Look at her. Are you proud of yourself now? You worried her to death."

Mrs. Chambers began to cry again, silently.

Carly searched his face. His eyes were dry. He was calm, in control again. But Carly felt a quiet resolve gaining strength within herself. Her decisions were made.

"I just needed time to think," she said, "about the lies you wanted me to tell."

His right eye twitched slightly, but he said nothing.

"And I decided..." Carly took a deep breath and willed herself not to look away from him. "I decided that I have to tell the truth." The words came tumbling out, hard and fast, and almost seemed to hit him in the face.

His fingers dug into the side of the mattress, but he spoke sweetly. "And what would that truth be?"

"That there was money in that candy box, row after row of it. It was counterfeit too, wasn't it?"

Mrs. Chambers was frozen, her mouth half open.

He merely smiled. "Ah, Carly. Is that what you think? You're only a child and you understand nothing. That was just payment of a business debt. It doesn't concern you. You don't have to lie. Just don't say anything.

Say you don't know."

Carly hugged her arms to her body. She had started this thing and she wasn't going to back down. "That's the same thing as lying. I'm not going to lie anymore."

"You'll do what I tell you to do and nothing else!" he thundered, punching a pillow to the bed.

"Carly, no!" Mrs. Chambers grabbed her daughter's arm. "You can't."

"Don't worry, Leila. No one will believe her, not after what she did." He stuffed the pillow back behind his head, confident. "Did you know that Carly pushed me off the roof? I kept quiet about it before, but I have to tell on her now. She's a troubled child, Leila. She needs professional help."

Mrs. Chambers let go of Carly's arm and took two steps backward.

"Mom?" Carly turned toward her mother. "You don't believe..."

"She hit me with a flashlight too." Mr. Chambers put his hands behind his head and a small smile played at the corners of his mouth. "You're so high and mighty, so interested in the truth," he scoffed. "Go ahead and tell your mother how you hit me."

"I did," Carly sputtered, "but only because..."

"See that? See that? She even admits it." He slapped his hand down on the side of the bed. "It could be you next, Leila. She's out of control. You know what her temper is like."

"Mom, I would never..."

"They'll just put her in a juvenile hall for a while,"

Mr. Chambers interrupted. "And after she's all straightened out, we'll go back and get her. It's for the best." He stared straight at his wife. "She tried to kill me, Leila."

"Mom! It wasn't like that! He slipped on some loose tiles. I tried to warn him, but he wouldn't believe me. Look! Look!" Carly began to peel the bandage from her arm. "I tried to hold on to him, to pull him back up," she cried, struggling with the tape. "The nail from the gutter got me." She ripped the tape off her arm and the bleeding began again. She started to cry. "I'm tired of lying about my bruises, about the things he does," she sobbed. "I'm tired of it. I just can't do it anymore."

Mrs. Chambers folded Carly into her arms. "Shhh. It's okay," she murmured, rocking her back and forth. "It'll be okay."

Mr. Chambers snorted. "It's just a show. Another one of her little plays for your attention, Leila. Your mother will testify with me, Carly. She probably even saw you push me. You need professional help. Doesn't she, Leila?"

Mrs. Chambers stopped rocking, but stood mute, her arms still wrapped around Carly. A tremble ran through her mother's body and Carly held her breath.

"Leila! You saw it, didn't you? You saw her push me."

Mrs. Chambers slowly raised her head. "I can't do it, Vinnie. I can't send her away."

He struggled to get out of the bed, but his IV line was wrapped around the rail and he winced from pain or anger. His face was a mottled shade of red, his eyes wild.

"Leila!" he hissed. "What are you talking about! They'll send you away! It's either her or us. At least she'll have someone to take care of her in a juvenile hall. What'll she do if we're gone? Did you think of that? Did you?" He was frantically working at the IV line, unhooking the bag from its metal stand.

"I can't do it, Vinnie," she whispered. "She's just a little girl. Please, Vinnie. Don't make me."

"There's no other way!" he shrieked. "What's the matter with you?"

He was on his feet now, and Mrs. Chambers seemed to shrink. She clutched Carly's shirt and they took several steps toward the door, arm in arm. "I'm taking her out now, Vinnie. She's bleeding."

"NO!" he screamed, ripping the IV line out of his arm. He stood beside the bed in his too small hospital gown, panting. "Don't you dare leave! Get back here!"

Mrs. Chambers paused, shaking, undecided. He saw his opening and tried again. "Leila, love, don't I always know what's best? Haven't I always taken care of you? I just want to do what's right for Carly. She pushed me off that roof. I could have died. She needs professional help."

Carly let go of her mother and stood on her own. She walked toward her father and stopped just in front of him. He was leaning on the end table, barefoot, his short hospital gown slipping off one shoulder, his face twisted and afraid. And for the first time, Carly saw him clearly. "You're wrong," she said, her voice calm and even. "You're the one who needs professional help. Not me." And she turned from him, took her mother's arm, and walked out of the room.

# CHAPTER 30

Carly waited in line at Rita's Water Ice on a Saturday that was dripping sun, just a touch of fall in the air off the ocean.

"Hey, Carly! What do you think?" Aileen did a little twirl behind the counter, showing off her pink T-shirt and white apron, a metal scoop in her hand.

Carly gave her a thumbs up. "You look great!"

Aileen had attempted to tie down her hair, but it was like trying to take the bloom out of a tree. Red coils sprouted all over her head and bobbed with her every move. She leaned across the counter to Carly. "It's only my second day, but so far, so good. I get paid next week. Alexa and I are saving up for a camping trip. Say, what do you want? Ice cream, water ice, gelati? You name it. I can make it all."

"Two cherry water ice. Eddie's supposed to be on a strict diet. He says the water ice is fat free."

Aileen rolled her eyes. "Coming right up."

Aileen filled two large cups to the brim, pushing away Carly's offered money. "My treat," she insisted.

She leaned across the counter again, ignoring the other customers. "So, you wanna come over my house tomorrow? Sandra actually let me buy some posters and I'm dying to hang them up."

"I can't tomorrow. But maybe after school on Monday. My grandmother is coming tomorrow."

"You mean the one from Florida?"

"Yeah. My mom's mother. I haven't seen her since I was really little." Carly's grandmother had been sending money the last few weeks, and now insisted on coming to stay with them and help out until Mrs. Chambers got back on her feet again.

"You are so lucky." Aileen pulled a piece of gum from her apron pocket and popped it in her mouth.

"I am?"

"Grandmothers are the best. They buy you all kinds of stuff, they cook whatever you want for dinner and they say yes to anything you ask them. Sandra's mom is so cool. The last time she came to visit..."

Stephanie Dalton bumped Aileen. "You going to wait on more than one customer per hour?" she sniffed, bending to scoop some blueberry slush into a small cup.

"I don't know. I'll think about it and get back to you on that," Aileen retorted. "I guess I better go," she whispered to Carly. "Don't forget about Monday after school."

Carly wandered back to the bench across from the newsstand and handed Eddie his water ice. He had an umbrella clipped to the back rest and cushions lined his seat. A cooler filled with carrot sticks and Diet Coke served as his end table and occasional foot rest.

231

Margo had bought him one of those little battery operated fans, and it sat beside him, all orange and green stripes, like a strange, huge bug.

"Thanks, Carly." He pulled a napkin from the cooler and tucked it in his collar.

Carly adjusted the pillow behind his back. "All you need now is a television set."

"I thought about it," Eddie answered between slurps, "but I have to keep my eye on the stand."

Eddie's doctor had warned him to cut back on his work schedule, and so he stayed out of the stand during the hottest hours of the day and reclined on the bench, keeping a close eye on the kids he hired to work for him.

"How's your mom doing, any better?" he asked.

Carly shrugged. "A little bit. She's working down at the church today, cooking with the Aid for Friends people." Carly's mother had seemed lost and broken after the arrests, like a baby bird fallen from the nest. She wandered the house, purposeless, staring out windows or gazing endlessly into a display of stale chocolates. They hardly spoke to each other in the beginning, not out of anger, but because words had deserted them. It was as though their relationship had moved to a foreign country, one without a dictator, and it was taking some time to learn the new language. But they were learning.

Just yesterday Carly told her mother how much she had hated the "maybe game." They didn't have money now to waste on restaurants or movies, but her mother made a pitcher of lemonade and they sat outside in the sun on two folding chairs doing nothing but spending time, healing wounds.

"And how's the stomach ulcer?" Eddie asked.

"Much better, now that she's taking the medicine every day." Carly rested her arm on Eddie's broad shoulder. "Thanks to you."

"Hey, I keep telling you, it wasn't me. You must have a fairy godmother."

Carly's mother had been diagnosed with the ulcer weeks ago, but medicine was expensive and money was tight. After the free samples ran out, she simply suffered through it. But after anonymous donations of cash started appearing in their mailbox, Carly filled the prescription on her own and insisted her mother take the pills. Carly suspected that Eddie and Margo were the fairy godmothers, but they denied it.

"Construction worker." Eddie nodded toward a man who had stopped to buy a paper.

"Forget it. Look at his feet." The man's shoes were caked with mud and his khaki pants had matching streaks of brown. "Construction workers don't wear shoes like that. I think he's a botanist who just came out of the marsh."

Eddie shook his head. The smile disappeared from his face and his hand dropped to his lap. The little plastic spoon rested on his leg, bleeding red. "Juvenile delinquent," he said quietly.

Carly turned to see Frankie striding up the boardwalk. "Reforming juvenile delinquent," she corrected. "It sounds better."

Eddie grunted. "He stole twenty bucks from me yesterday. I saw him take it." He glanced down at his watch. "Well, at least he's starting to show up on time."

Frankie shuffled up to the stand and waited, scowling, while the girl he was relieving gathered up her things. He pulled a racing magazine from one of the racks and slumped onto the stool, slowly turning the pages, never once looking up at Eddie.

"You didn't tell him yet, did you?" Carly asked.

"No. I did not tell him yet. And you're going to give me another heart attack if you don't let up."

"But he should know."

"I'm just waiting a little bit. Hoping he gets to like me some before I spring the news on him."

Carly sighed. "Good luck."

"Yeah, well, at least he's past the name calling stage. I think we're making some progress."

Carly watched Frankie take change from a customer and drop the coins in the bucket. Plink. Plink. She remembered their struggle over that same bucket weeks ago, and the sound of hundreds of coins hitting the boardwalk all at once.

"I'll be right back." Carly grabbed her water ice and walked over to the stand. "You want this?" she asked.

Frankie glared at her. "What, and get dork germs from you? Forget it."

"I didn't eat any of it yet. I just thought you might get kind of hot in there."

Frankie dropped his chin into his hand. "Yeah. It's only like 150 degrees." He pulled the cup toward him and Carly stood back in case he decided to fling it in her direction. But he stirred the slush around and began to eat it.

The stand looked better than ever. The boardwalk merchants, led by Margo, had chipped in and given it a fresh coat of blue paint and a new door as a surprise for Eddie when he got out of the hospital.

Frankie looked up suddenly. "Hey, how's your jail-bird mother and father?"

Carly stiffened and felt the color rising to her face. The whole town knew her life story thanks to the local paper. Her father's counterfeiting, arrest, and failure to make bail, her deliveries, his fall from the roof; it was all there. Her life, in black and white, digested all across town with the morning coffee, like a gooey pastry.

She learned that the truth carried its own pains. Her life, always hidden by the lies and the darkness, was now unburied. And it came out bruised and embarrassingly ugly in places. But she refused to go back underground.

She leaned on the stand and answered Frankie in a clear voice. "None of your business. But, for your information, my mother is not in prison. She's just got to do community service. Kind of like you, don't you think?"

"Hey, this is a job!" Frankie insisted. "I get paid for being here. This ain't no community service."

He dug his spoon into the water ice. "You have to go to court or anything?"

Carly waited for the punch line, the sarcastic jab. But there was none. "No," she answered. "I don't have to go." The police didn't need her help after all. The old man on Bay Avenue had given them all the proof they needed. His name was Mr. Franco, and he had started out as an accomplice, a gambling buddy her father had met in Atlantic City. The two of them and Mr. Reese, the cigarette-smoking, barefoot man from Pacific Avenue, would shop with the counterfeit money all over the area. They paid for small things with big bills and got real money in change from unsuspecting store owners. They met frequently to divide up the real cash, her father getting the biggest share, and to exchange the names of the businesses they hit, always making sure that they never visited the same store twice. With nothing more than a computer, a scanner, and a color copier, her father had managed to make a lot of phony money and to fool a lot of people.

But Mr. Franco got caught buying a paperback novel in Elkart's Drug Emporium with a hundred dollar bill. Mrs. Elkart was seventy-six years old, and even though her eyesight wasn't the best, she could sense that something wasn't right and she hated to be cheated.

Mr. Franco decided to make a deal, to help catch the others in hopes of a lighter prison sentence for himself. But Mr. Chambers soon got suspicious and decided to pack up and make a quick move out of Oceanside. His fall from the roof put an end to that.

So when Carly returned to the hospital from the park, ready to talk about the deliveries she made and the money in the box, the police weren't even interested. They had treated her kindly and gently, and didn't ask her a single question about the money.

Carly felt a tap on her shoulder and turned to find Nick, his baseball cap in his hand, a smudge of pizza sauce on the front of his white T-shirt. A group of kids stood a few feet behind him, waiting, Jeff Connelly leaning on his boogie board.

"We're going to the beach, but I didn't want to go without you," Nick said.

Frankie rolled his eyes.

"Can you come?"

Before she could answer, Josh Manly stepped toward the stand. "Hey, newspaper boy!" he called to Frankie. "What's the headline today?" Josh looked back at the gang for their approving smiles and heard a few giggles. "Aren't you supposed to yell, 'read all about it!' or 'hear ye, hear ye,' or something? C'mon newspaper boy, let's hear it."

Frankie looked up slowly from his water ice. "Okay, Manly. Here's a news flash for you." He pulled back on the tip of his spoon and catapulted a blob of water ice at Josh. It hit Manly smack in the face, splattering into his hair and dribbling down his shirt.

Manly cursed and wiped his face with the back of his arm. "You jerk. You're dead, Frankie. Just you wait!" he screamed.

Frankie snorted and went back to eating what was left of the water ice.

"Let's get out of here," Nick suggested.

Carly watched the fuming Josh rubbing his face with the bottom of his shirt. She looked past him at the rest of the kids. Some of them smiled at her, some looked away. "I don't know," Carly said. "Maybe I shouldn't."

Nick followed her gaze. "I mean just you and me. We can catch up with them later." Nick turned to the gang of kids. "I'll see you guys later. Carly and I are going to hang out for a while."

There were some whistles and raised eyebrows, but he ignored them. He put his hand in hers and they started toward the beach.

"Carly!" Frankie called to her and she turned. His arms were resting on a stack of newspapers, his thin lips stained cherry red, just the hint of a smile forming at the edges. "Thanks for the water ice."

Carly smiled back at him. "Anytime."

With a wave to Eddie, she and Nick took off for the beach, the day beach. The ocean rolled toward her, gulls swooping low, the sand warm beneath her feet. There were lifeguards in the lifeguard stands, but she didn't mind a bit. She walked along the water's edge with Nick, dodging Frisbees and squealing toddlers, joggers and dripping swimmers. The day beach was full of colors, bright bathing suits and striped trunks, buckets, shovels, boats and blankets, golden yellow sun and green blue ocean.

Nick hopped over a small wave, and splashed some water on his arms and down the back of his neck. "How was practice yesterday?"

"It was okay." Nick had talked her into trying out for the track team at school and she had made it. There was something about running that she had always loved, when her whole body was in perfect rhythm, pushing hard, the ground sliding away beneath her feet. And now, it was even better. She wasn't running away anymore, but forward, toward the finish line.

"What do you mean 'okay'?" Nick argued. "I heard you were awesome."

"Who said that?"

"Everybody. Word gets around, you know."

Carly smiled. She had been good. She beat Catherine Cooke, one of the school's best runners, in the 440. "We have our first indoor meet in a couple of weeks. You wanna come?"

Nick shook his head. "Nah. I don't think so."

"What?!" Carly knocked his cap off and it flipped into the ocean. "After all those boring baseball games I sat through? You better be there."

Nick shook the water off his cap, laughing. "I'm kidding. I'm kidding," he sang. "You know I'm going to be there."

"Hey, look!" Carly bent and picked up something shining in the surf.

Nick fingered it. "Sea glass," he said.

It was a piece of a broken bottle, thick and sparkling, its sharp edges all worn smooth by time and the ocean. It was beautiful. Carly held it up to the sun. "Wow. Just think of everything this glass must have gone through to get here like this."

Nick took the piece in his hand and squeezed it. "Probably a lot. It's still pretty strong too." He dropped it in Carly's open palm. "I think you should start a collection."

She closed her fingers around the sea glass. "Maybe I will."

Carly turned and looked out toward the horizon. The sun was dancing on the water and a warm breeze played through her hair. She felt as though her whole life had opened up. It was stretched out before her like the wide expanse of the ocean, unpredictable, but suddenly full of possibilities.

"Come on!" She called to Nick.

And she dashed out into the water and dived right in.